Daddy Drinks

THERESA HELEN CHANNELL

Outskirts Press, Inc.
Denver, Colorado

Daddy Drinks
All Rights Reserved.
Copyright © 2011 Theresa Helen Channell
V4.0

Outskirts Press, Inc.
http://www.outskirtspress.com

PB ISBN: 978-1-4327-3011-6
HB ISBN: 978-1-4327-3012-3

Library of Congress Control Number: 2010921784

Outskirts Press and the "OP" logo are trademarks belonging to Outskirts Press, Inc.

PRINTED IN THE UNITED STATES OF AMERICA

To my grandma,

Helen Mary Gates, my godmother,

For always believing in me...your unconditional love

kept me going during my "blue" days.

Don't stop praying for me...

I love you!

Alicia Marie Zamarelli...

That's my name. Momma and Daddy call me Lissy. My best friend Megan calls me Zammy. The rude boys in my fifth-grade class at school call me Zamboni (like the machine used to smooth the ice at the hockey arena). They think they're so clever. I like hockey so it doesn't bother me, but they don't know that. Boys are stupid sometimes.

My dad is the lead guitarist in a rock band. He's lean and tall with hazel eyes and medium length light brown hair that starts to curl when it gets long. I tease him sometimes as we look at old pictures of him and Uncle Matt when they first started singing together. They both had really long hair and wore costumes instead of the jeans and t-shirts they wear now.

Uncle Matt is taller than Dad, with dark brown hair and amazingly blue eyes. He and Dad work out at the gym every day so they can keep their "girlish figures." That's what my dad says. He's so silly.

Uncle Matt and Dad have been best friends since they were teenagers. They've been famous ever since I can remember - ten years at least. That's how old I am.

Momma is an actress. She's absolutely gorgeous with long blonde hair and brown eyes. I hope I look half as good as she does when I grow up.

Me, I'm tall for my age. I think I'm too skinny. Momma says I'm at that "awkward age," whatever that means. Daddy says I'm Mom's "Mini Me," like in the movie *Austin Powers*, because she and I look so much alike, only my eyes are hazel like his.

Momma travels a lot for work, but right now she's working in L.A., so I get to go to my old school and spend time with Megan. That's cool.

There are always reporters and ***paparazzi**** hanging around waiting to take pictures of Mom and Dad. I just smile and wait for them to go away. It can be annoying at times.

My parents got divorced recently, and I cried a lot in the beginning. I was afraid I wouldn't be able to see my dad since I have to live with my mom. I really want to live with my dad, but Momma says she'd miss me too much.

Momma has been taking a prescription drug for depression since before she filed for divorce. Sometimes she also has a few drinks with her pills (even though the instructions on the bottle say not to). Then she falls asleep, and I end up all by myself. I hate that.

The depression is not the only reason my parents got divorced. I can't share any information about the

---

***Paparazzi** are photographers that follow celebrities around waiting to take pictures of them in their public and private activities.*

reasons because Grandmama says it's no one's business but our own.

Today my dad is coming home to spend spring break with me after being gone for two weeks. Woohoo! I can't wait to see him. This time he went to New York City, Chicago, Detroit, and Nashville.

Dad calls or texts me from wherever he is working. I can contact him anytime I want, except when he's in concert. That's usually after my bedtime anyway, so it's not a problem.

Megan and I are going shopping with my mom this morning, and then, in the afternoon, Dad will be picking us up with his new girlfriend Tracey. She writes children's books. Dad met her in New York City after one of his concerts, and he seems to really like her.

Tracey's got sun-streaked brown hair and incredibly blue eyes. She's a little taller than Momma, but my dad still stands a good seven inches above her.

I like spending time with her because she's always smiling and laughing.

Anyway, we'll be spending the next week at the beach or just hanging out at Dad's house, which is just down the street from Megan's house.

Well, at least that was the plan...

Daddy Gets Arrested

Megan and I were sitting with Tracey in a little cubicle the police officers called "an office," and our moms were on their way to take us home. We had gone to the movies and were driving home when the nightmare began.

It was close to midnight. Megan and I were wide awake from all the Coke® we drank that evening. Dad's cell phone rang, and when he tried to answer it, he dropped it. Reaching down to get it, his foot slipped off the brake, and the car rolled into the intersection without stopping. Dad pulled off to the curb to avoid any cars that might be coming and picked up his phone.

Two police squad cars happened to be sitting at that very corner and pulled up behind our car with their lights flashing. The sirens scared us, and Daddy swore out loud, "Great! This is just what I need to cap off a perfect evening!"

Mom and Dad had argued for a long time when he came to pick Megan and me up earlier in the day. Dad seemed sad after we left her house. I wish they wouldn't fight. I like it when Dad is happy because he is a lot more fun to be with.

I would like to forget about the whole DUI incident. The police officers came up to the car and asked for Dad's driver's license, car registration, and proof of insurance. He had to blow into a **breathalyzer®***. Then they made him get out of the car. He had to touch the tip of his nose with his finger and say the alphabet backwards.

*A **breathalyzer®** (breath analyzer) is a device used to estimate the amount of alcohol in someone's blood by taking a breath sample.*

Next thing I knew, one of the officers put hand-cuffs on my dad's wrists. I got out and tried to stop him, but Daddy told me to get back in the car. I was scared and started to cry. I held on to my dad's leg until the police officers pulled me off and then made Daddy get into one of the squad cars.

One of the officers told me that everything would be all right. He said they were taking my dad to the police station and would call my mom to come and get me. But I didn't understand.

"Why are you taking my dad to jail? He's not a criminal."

Officer Logan handed me a tissue and sat me on the back seat of the second squad car. "Your dad drank too much alcohol tonight and drove his car while he was intoxicated. That's against the law."

I sniffed, and wiping the tears from my cheeks asked, "What's intoxicated?"

Patiently, the officer explained the word

"intoxicated" to me. "It's when a person has consumed (drunk) enough alcohol to impair (mess up) his or her reaction time and judgment."

"Will he have to stay in jail for a long time?"

"That's up to the judge." Officer Logan smiled kindly as he buckled my seatbelt for me. Then he went to get Megan and Tracey. Tracey didn't want to drive Dad's car because she had had a few drinks, too.

After locking Dad's car, we rode to the police station in the squad car. Tracey was really nice and stayed with us until our moms came so we wouldn't be scared. "I'll make sure your dad gets home okay," she promised.

When my mom arrived, she freaked out, as usual. She looked me over front-and-back, top-to-bottom. "Alicia, are you all right?" She didn't even ask about Dad. I wanted to see him, but no one would let me. I cried all the way home and begged my mom to get Dad out of jail.

The Morning After

The next morning, Dad sent me a text message on my cell phone to see if I was okay. I called him back, and we talked for a long time. He said he was sorry for what had happened and promised that it would never happen again.

My dad never makes a promise he can't keep – NEVER. I told him I believed him and asked when he was coming to get me. Spring break was supposed to be *our* time together. He said he would see me later that morning because he had to make some phone calls to take care of the "incident." That's what he calls it whenever the subject is brought up now.

When Dad got to Mom's house, they argued

forever. I tried to stay in my room, but they started screaming at each other, and I couldn't stand it any longer. Running into the living room, I shouted out loudly, "PLEASE STOP SCREAMING AT EACH OTHER!"

Mom scowled at me while Dad raised an eyebrow and pointed his finger at me. I stopped dead in my tracks. Dad only did the raised eyebrow/finger gesture when he was really mad. I tried asking them again using my inside voice, "Please…stop screaming."

Dad turned back to my mom, "She's mine for the week, Katelynn."

"You got arrested for DUI, Joey."

"I'm not DUI now." Pointing toward my bedroom, Dad said, "Lissy, go get your bag."

I turned and ran back to my room to get my things. Momma followed me. "I want you to call me if you need to come home, Lissy. If Daddy has too many drinks, you call me. Do you understand?" I looked up at her, then to my father who had just entered my bedroom behind us.

"She won't *need* to call you, Katelynn. I'm not going to be drinking anymore."

"I've heard that before."

They were at it again. "I'm ready, Daddy," I interrupted as I picked up my backpack and hurried past them to Dad's car. I didn't want to hear them arguing anymore.

The ride to my dad's house was quiet. I had so many questions I wanted to ask him, but I didn't want to make him angry. Looking out the window, I thought to myself, *"I wish I had someone I could talk to."* Turning toward my father, I finally got up the courage to ask, "Daddy, what's DUI?"

He took a deep breath and held it for a moment before exhaling loudly. I thought he was mad at me when he pulled the car over to the side of the road, shifted into park, and looked back at me. "DUI is an acronym for driving under the influence of alcohol or drugs.”

“What’s an acronym?” I scrunched up my face as I looked at him.

“Acronyms are abbreviations using initials in a phrase or name. ‘AMZ’ would be the acronym for your full name.”

I thought for a moment, “Oh…like ‘BLT’ for a bacon, lettuce, and tomato sandwich?”

“You got it, Baby,” Daddy smiled and winked at me.

“The police officer said you broke the law last night.”

Dad sighed and stared out the windshield. “Yes, I did.” He turned toward me, his eyes shining, “I’m sorry, Sweetie. I should have used the brains God gave me. It’ll never happen again.”

“I didn’t mean to make you cry, Daddy.” I was starting to get tears in my eyes again. I hate crying. It makes your nose run, and there's never a tissue when you need one.

"I love you, Lissy. I'd never let anything happen to you. You know that, right?"

"Yes, Daddy." I unbuckled my seatbelt and crawled up to the front and onto his lap. He held me close and kissed the top of my head.

"It's gonna be okay," he promised again.

I Wonder

Megan was sitting on the front porch when we got to my dad's house. I didn't really feel like playing with her right then, but Dad told me he needed some time alone to think. I told Megan to wait outside as I followed my dad into the house with my bag.

"I want to spend time with *you,* Daddy."

"Sweetie, Daddy told you he needs some time alone. Go play with Megan; I'll call you when it's time to come home for dinner."

I gave him a big hug before dropping my bag by the front door. "Hey!" Dad called out to me. "Does that belong there?"

Looking up at him, I couldn't tell if he was mad, or not. He had his "stern dad" look going, but he was smiling, too. "Sorry, Daddy." I picked up the bag and ran to my room to place it on the chest at the foot of my bed. Dad stood in the doorway.

"You can unpack your stuff later. Now get out of here, you little monkey!" He swatted my behind as I raced past him. It didn't hurt though. My dad never spanks me. He just gives me "reminders" of what *could* happen if I don't behave.

I turned back and hugged him as hard as I could. "I love you, Dad."

Megan was standing in the hallway with her hands on her hips. "For the love of God, you people hug more than anybody I know. Could we please go to my house *now*, Zammy?"

I turned and laughed. I don't think Megan's parents hug or kiss her much. We held hands as we walked to her house.

"Are your parents angry?" I asked when we were out of earshot from my dad.

"Not really. They said it could have happened to any-one. My parents drive after they drink all the time."

I stopped her and looked around before continu-ing the conversation, "Did you know it's against the law to drive after you drink?"

"Duh, they told us that in D.A.R.E at school, remember?"

"Yeah, but this is different. This time it was my dad. I don't want any of the other kids to know, Megan."

"Zammy, there's no way they won't know. Your mom and dad are famous. It'll be all over the place – in the newspapers, magazines, on TV..."

She put her hands on my shoulders and slowly looked around us. "They could be watching us... RIGHT NOW!" she yelled into my ear and then ran ahead of me when I swung at her for scaring me.

"You are such a brat!" I chased after her. We both

stopped suddenly when her mom came out the front door.

"How's your father, Lissy?" Mrs. Jensen turned away from me before I could answer. She does that all the time. I'm kind of used to it. Besides, I didn't want to talk to her about my dad anyway.

"Megan, there are leftovers in the fridge for dinner. I'll be home after midnight. Don't stay up too late." She got into her Mercedes-Benz® and, without another word, backed out of the driveway and drove off.

"Cool, we've got the house to ourselves." Megan opened the front door, and we stepped inside out of the warm California sunshine.

"Megan, where's Marianna?" Marianna was the housekeeper who spent a lot of time babysitting Megan.

"She went to the grocery store to pick up the food for Mom and Dad's party. Hey! You want to see something?" I followed Megan downstairs to the "party" room. The Jensens had a finished walkout basement. They threw parties nearly every weekend. Some were classier than others.

The basement was decked out in *Cinco de Mayo** decorations. Mrs. Jensen liked theme parties. There were dozens of sombreros sitting on the bar, and a piñata was waiting to be hung outside on the covered patio.

Megan went behind the bar and brought out some miniature bottles. "Check these out; aren't they cute?" There were bottles of Kahlúa®, Mezcal®, Acachú®, Damiana Orange Liquor®, and lots of other drinks.

"What's li-quor?" I was having a hard time reading the tiny labels.

*Cinco de Mayo (Spanish for "Fifth of May") is celebrated in honor of Mexico's victory in the Battle of Puebla on May 5, 1862. The date is voluntarily observed in the United States and other locations around the world as a celebration of Mexican heritage and pride.

"Not li-quor; it's pronounced licker."

I picked up another bottle and read the label, "Cabo Wabo®?"

"That's tequila!" Megan grabbed the bottle from me. "Sometimes there's a worm on the bottom of the bottle. This one doesn't have one." She turned the bottle upside down in case the worm was hidden in the cap. "That's 'cuz it's not 110 proof." She put the bottles back behind the bar.

"One hundred ten proof?" I looked at her puzzled.

"Yeah, don't you know anything?"

I shook my head and waited for her to dazzle me with her knowledge. Megan liked to prove she was smarter than me. I didn't mind. I learned a lot of new stuff from her.

"Proof is how strong the liquor is." She picked up another bottle and showed me. "See here?" She pointed to the tiny writing at the bottom of the label.

"This one is 40 proof." She grabbed another. "This one is stronger; it's 80 proof."

"*How* do you know this?" I asked, amazed at her knowledge of alcohol anything. "And *why*?"

"Oh, I was reading the label on a bottle one day and asked my dad about it. He told me to use the Internet to look it up. He always does that when he doesn't want to be bothered, which is most of the time!" She laughed as she put the bottle down, and we walked outside to sit on the patio.

"Megan, do you ever wonder what it feels like to be intoxicated?"

"I *know* what it feels like." She smiled at me with a weird look on her face.

"What do you mean?" I looked at her suspiciously.

"I drank some of my mom's champagne last New Year's Eve. She didn't even know; she was so wasted."

I started to get nervous as Megan recounted the many times she had *tried* her mother's drinks. She described the difference between wine and liquor. She even knew the proofs of all the alcohol in her dad's beer collection.

I was glad when my dad called me home for dinner. I didn't want to know so much about alcohol. I didn't think it was a good idea for Megan to know so much either, but I kept my thoughts to myself.

Marianna arrived just as I was leaving. I greeted her as I walked down the driveway, "Buenas noches, Marianna!"

"Buenas noches, Miss Zammy!" Marianna started unloading the car.

"I'll call you later!" Megan yelled at me while holding the door open for Marianna.

Daddy's Place

We had Schezuan for dinner; it's one of my favorites. If Dad was trying to make it up to me for the night before, it was definitely working. After dinner, we snuggled next to each other in the living room while listening to music.

"Did you have fun at Megan's?"

"Not really; it was boring."

"Are you bored now?"

I rolled my eyes. "No, Daddy, I'm NEVER bored with you!" We both laughed out loud.

"Daddy, are you going to see Tracey again?"

"Why do you ask?"

"I like her; she's really nice."

Dad shifted sideways and looked at me. "What?"

I tried to look innocent.

"You really like her?"

"Yes, Dad, I do."

"Well, maybe I'll give her a call later."

"Why not call her now?" I picked up his cell phone from the coffee table and handed it to him.

"What, are you playing matchmaker?" Daddy set his phone back on the table.

"No, Dad. She's really nice. You seemed so happy last night when you were with her, and she made sure Megan and I felt safe. I…uh…I just really like her. Don't you?"

Dad was smiling down at me as he listened. "I'll call her after you go to bed." He looked at his watch and stood up. Reaching down for my hands, he swung me up onto his shoulders. He hadn't done that in a long time.

"Dad, don't hurt yourself."

"A little less noise from the peanut gallery."

"Megan's supposed to call me."

"You can talk to Megan tomorrow. Right now, it's bedtime."

"Okay." I wrapped my hands under his chin and held on as he headed toward my bedroom, ducking as we passed through the doorway.

After brushing my teeth, I changed into my pajamas and then knelt by the side of my bed to say my prayers.

I asked God to please help my dad and mom stop fighting and drinking. "…and God, thank You for blessing Uncle Matt and his family – oh, and Daddy's new girlfriend Tracey. Amen."

I didn't notice that my dad had opened the door and heard my prayers, but I heard him quietly close the door. Then he knocked before coming in to tuck me in for the night. I kissed and hugged him really hard, so he'd know how much I loved him.

"Tell Tracey I said 'thank you' when you talk to her. Okay?"

"I will."

"Sing a song to me, Daddy."

"*Now?*"

"Please?"

"What song do you want to hear?"

"*My* song!"

Daddy sang the song that he had written for me when I was a baby. I drifted off to sleep before the song ended.

Uncle Matt

The next morning, I awoke to the music of Dad's band on my cell phone. It was Uncle Matt. We talked for a while and he promised to come and visit before the end of the week.

When he mentioned "the incident," I paused before explaining to him what had happened that night. "Daddy and Tracey had drinks at dinner, Uncle Matt. We went to the movies, and he was driving us home when the police arrested him."

"I didn't ask about that Lissy; I asked about *you*. How are *you* doing?"

"I'm fine, Uncle Matt. Really!"

Matthew Alan James is the founder and lead

singer of the band MAJIC. He's also my godfather and my best grown-up friend. Uncle Matt has always been easy to talk to. He has never spoken to my dad about any of our conversations without my permission. Usually he convinces me to talk to Dad about my problems myself after I confide in him.

I can talk to Uncle Matt about anything – usually. But today I couldn't talk to him. I was still confused about my feelings and didn't want to discuss them with him. I was…embarrassed. I wanted to talk to my dad about "the incident" but was afraid I'd make him sad again. I didn't want to make him cry. It scared me to see him crying the other day. Dads don't cry, right?

So, I avoided talking to Uncle Matt about "the incident" and asked him about the tour and how things were going at his house. "How's Aunt Gabriella? Any new tour dates? What's going on with Tammy, Steven, Nicky, and Jacob? What day did you say you're coming to visit Dad and me?"

He caught the drift and interrupted me. "Lissy, if you need to talk, you have my number."

I paused for a moment and thought about discussing my feelings with him, then decided against it. "We can talk about it when you get here, Uncle Matt. Okay?"

I heard him sigh as he reluctantly agreed, "Okay, I love you, Sweet Girl."

"I love you, too, Uncle Matt." We said our goodbyes, and I pushed the disconnect button just as my dad knocked on my bedroom door.

"Good morning, Monkey." He was smiling, and before I could maneuver out of the way, he started tickling me.

"Daddy! Stop! Please!" I begged, but he kept on. "I'm gonna pee my pants!" I yelled and pushed his hands from my stomach. Laughing, he picked me up and carried me to the bathroom.

"I've been able to walk since I was eleven months old, you know?" I looked him in the eyes, and he winked at me as he set me down.

"I miss carrying you."

"Dad, contrary to popular belief, I am *not* a monkey. You really need to get over that." I closed the bathroom door in his still grinning face.

"You're *my* monkey," he said through the door.

"What...ever!" I said in my best "valley girl" voice.

Heart-to-Heart

After breakfast, Dad and I took a ride down to the beach. We walked along the water, and I collected sea shells for the millionth time.

"Dad..." I wanted to talk to him but hesitated. There were so many things I needed to know.

"What is it, Baby?" He looked concerned. I pulled on his hand to get him to kneel so I could speak with him face-to-face.

"Yesterday, Momma said the judge might change his ruling and not let you have joint custody of me." I started to cry and fell into his open arms as the tears turned into uncontrollable sobs. I hadn't meant to bring up the subject, but I was scared and needed to know where I stood with my dad. It was bad enough that my parents had gotten divorced the year before, but what if my mother was right? What if I couldn't see my dad anymore?

I heard Daddy swear under his breath. He held me close as he sat down on the warm sand, pulling me into his embrace. I felt safe and warm. He kissed me on the top of the head over and over again, promising that he would never let that happen. "I'll always be there for you, Lissy – always."

"You said you don't make promises you can't keep." I turned to look up at him.

As he wiped away my tears using his shirt sleeve, he looked confused. "What do you mean?"

"You still smoke, Dad. Grandpa smoked; look what happened to him."

I did a paper on lung disease for school. Grandpa Zamarelli died last year from lung cancer; that's why I chose that particular subject. I wanted to understand what caused my grandpa to get cancer and how to prevent my dad from getting it, too.

"How did we get on this subject? Lissy, I'm not going to get cancer."

"Dad!"

"Okay, okay. I'll try to quit again."

"You gave it up for Lent, Dad. Just because Lent is over doesn't mean you have to start again. Please, Daddy?" I got up from his lap and turned to take his face in my hands. "I don't want to lose you." I thought for a moment. "You know, Dad, Tracey doesn't smoke."

"Tracey?"

"Did you call her last night?"

"What's Tracey got to do with this?"

I ignored him. "Did you?"

He smirked at me. "Yes, as a matter of fact, I did."

"Cool!"

"That's it? No more questions?"

"Nope. Except…you *are* going to see her again, right?"

"For your information, she's on a book-signing tour and won't be back for a few weeks."

"Daddy! She agreed to see you, right?"

"I'm meeting her in New York City after you go back to your mom's. Is that okay with you?"

"Terrific! Now where were we? Oh yeah, you were gonna *promise* not to smoke anymore."

"I was?" Dad's eyebrow went up.

"Yes, Daddy, you were."

My dad promised to stop smoking for good. I *made* him promise.

We took his cigarettes and tore them into a ba-zillion pieces before throwing the pack in the trash can.

Next, he drove to the drug store to pick up a supply of **nicotine*** gum. Daddy made a funny face when he put a piece in his mouth, causing me to laugh out loud. "Yuck!" he said. He made another face at me in the rearview mirror as he chewed while driving us home.

After lunch, Dad sent me down to Megan's so he could make a few phone calls. "You're not going to call Momma, are you?" He looked guilty. "Please, Daddy. Momma will get mad at me for telling you. She doesn't know that I...uh..."

"Overheard a private conversation?" he finished for me. Both eyebrows rose this time.

*****Nicotine** is a stimulant to mammals; it's the main factor responsible for tobacco smoking addiction, which is one of the hardest addictions to break. Nicotine gum is used to help people slowly wean themselves off the addictive substance.*

"I didn't mean to." I clung to his shirttail as he calmly tried to get me to leave the house so I could enjoy the beautiful day outdoors with my friend.

"I won't call her today; I promise."

"You sure are making a lot of promises, Dad," I laughed. "I'm gonna get a bulletin board and write them down so you don't forget."

"Go!" He playfully pushed me out the front door. I stuck my tongue out at him, and he pretended to chase after me as I ran, laughing down the street to Megan's house.

"Just wait 'til you get home later!" Dad shook his finger at me jokingly before heading back inside the house. I wasn't afraid. I knew he wouldn't do anything to hurt me.

Disobeying My Parents

Megan's mom *and* dad were home. Joy! I didn't mind them usually, but they were both drinking, and her mom made a comment about my dad that I didn't understand at all. She called him a "lush," whatever that means. I planned to look the word up when I got home. Mr. Jensen apologized for her and shooed Megan and me outside to play.

"Megan, how long have they been drinking this time?"

"Since breakfast…Mom had a mimosa, and Dad drank something black and icky looking to get rid of his hangover."

We both sighed deeply as we sat on the front porch

steps staring blankly into space. Despite our cares, it was a beautiful day; the sun was shining, and a cool breeze was blowing in from the Pacific Ocean.

"Want to go for a bike ride?" Megan got up and raced toward the garage.

"Sure! I'll run home and get my bike." I jumped up to leave.

"Wait, I'll go with you." Megan rode her bike next to me as we headed back to my dad's house.

The sun seemed to sink behind a cloud as I noticed my mom's car parked in the driveway. She was throwing my stuff in the trunk and yelling at my dad. We stopped before she or my dad saw us and quickly turned back toward Megan's house.

"I'll get my bike later." I was disgusted with my parents. "Dad will take care of whatever is freaking her out."

Megan stood up. "Hop on the seat of my bike, Zammy." We rode double down the street and around the corner before my mother turned and started walking toward the Jensen's house.

"KATELYNN, YOU'RE BEING UNREASONABLE!" That was the last thing I heard Daddy yell as we ducked behind the tree on the corner and watched my parents fighting in public.

I looked around for paparazzi and slapped Megan's arm when she pretended to snap a photo with an imaginary camera. "Stop it, Megan. That's not funny!" Blinking back tears, I tried to keep them from falling and turned away so she wouldn't tease me.

"Hey, Zammy, I'm sorry. I won't make fun of them. Come on, let's go down to the beach and watch the surfers."

I rolled my eyes. "I'm not allowed to go to the beach without my mom or dad, remember?"

"Don't you do anything you're not allowed to do?" I thought she was kidding, but Megan was absolutely serious.

"No, I like the fact that I can brag and say I've never been spanked in my life. Do you *like* it when your parents punish you?"

"Well, no…but it sure is fun until they do." Megan laughed out loud and started to leave without me.

"Terrorist!" I teased her.

"Anarchist!" she yelled back.

"What the heck is an anarchist?"

"I don't know, but it sounds bad."

"I'll have to look it up later."

I glanced once more at my parents as they fought in the distance, and then I looked back at Megan. She seemed so confident; nothing seemed to scare her. I wished I was more like her. She was two inches taller than me with long brown hair and steel blue eyes. She would never have to go through the "awkward age" like me, and she looked great with her perfect Coppertone® tan. I have to admit it: I was a little jealous of her.

Megan stopped to look back at me. "Are you coming, or not?"

"Hmm, we'd only stay for a little while?"

"Absolutely!"

"Okay, but my parents can't ever find out."

"All right, Zammy's breaking free of the parental chains! Let's go!"

We decided to forget about my bike, and I rode the three miles to the beach on Megan's. It was almost all downhill. I held on to her for dear life, expecting to crash at any moment. She laughed at me, pedaling all the faster.

"Megan, slow down!" The wind was whipping my hair into my eyes, and I couldn't see where we were going, which was a good thing because I was terrified by her recklessness.

Megan managed to make it through all of the stop lights, never using the brakes once! We wiped out when the front tire sank into the sand, bringing us to an abrupt stop. We both flew from the bike. I tumbled several times, scraping my hands, elbows, and knees. "Megan!" I yelled at her but then started giggling when I saw that she was laughing so hard she had tears in her eyes. "How am I going to explain *this* to my parents?"

Her laughter turned to mild concern. "Your chin is bleeding." That's all she said as she led the way to the girl's bathroom. I tried to clean up my wounds and ended up taking a shower on the boardwalk to get the sand off of me. We sat on one of the benches while my clothes dried.

"Not one of your brightest ideas." I glared at her while blowing softly on my knees to try to ease the throbbing pain.

"Next time, we'll make sure you have your own bike. We wouldn't have crashed if we'd been on separate bikes."

"Who says there's gonna be a next time?" She just

smiled at me - what a brat!

My cell phone played out the familiar ringtone that let me know it was my dad calling. "Oh no! I am going to be in so much trouble!"

"Don't answer it!" Megan grabbed my phone from me. As she handed it back, she advised, "Just tell your dad you forgot to charge it."

"That's lying." I couldn't believe she had actually suggested that I lie to my father. Unbelievable!

"Well, do you still want to be able to brag that you've never been spanked?"

Oh Lord, why had I listened to her? I should have said NO, but I didn't want to go home and listen to my parents arguing. Now what was I gonna do?

I let the ringtone play until it stopped. Then I opened my phone and turned the ring volume to off. Megan looked at me cock-eyed. "I'll tell him that my ringer was turned off."

"Good idea; I've taught you well." Megan slapped

me on the back and put her arm around my shoulders before we started the long walk back to her house, dragging her bike behind us.

I'd never walked three miles before, at least not all at one time. It was hard work trudging uphill in the middle of the afternoon with the hot sun beating down on us. We were almost to our street when my dad flew around the corner in his car. He slammed on the brakes and jumped out when he saw us.

"Where have you been, Young Lady?" He was mad, madder than I had ever seen him. Or was he scared? I couldn't tell. When I didn't answer, he looked at Megan and raised an eyebrow in disapproval. I closed my eyes expecting the worst. When I opened my eyes, my dad did the eyebrow thingy looking right at me. I knew I was gonna be grounded – or worse, spanked.

Megan used her sweet little girl voice, "Hello, Mr. Zamarelli."

"Megan, what happened to Lissy?" Dad asked,

looking me over like my mom had at the police station. He was assessing the damage and eyeing the blood on my chin and knees. "*What* happened to you?"

"We had an accident, Mr. Z."

"I can see that, Megan." Daddy turned back toward me. "Lissy, Honey, are you okay?"

Megan pushed me from behind, knocking the wind from my lungs. I stumbled forward and Dad caught me before I hit the pavement. "Oh, Baby!" He picked me up and carried me to his car. Looking back over his shoulder, I watched as Megan smiled and winked up at me.

When we got to my dad's house, he carried me into the bathroom. "Daddy, really I'm okay. It's just a few scratches."

"It's *not* just a few scratches. For God's sake, what happened to you?"

"We were riding Megan's bike."

"Together?" Dad interrupted. "On Megan's bike? Lissy, you know better than that."

He left me to clean myself up after running a bath for me. The warm water stung as I slowly lowered myself into the tub. I used the soap and washcloth Dad left me to clean my wounds. It really hurt, but I forced myself to rub all of the dirt off as "penance for my sins."

"Almost done?" Dad asked through the door.

"Yes, Daddy; I just have to wash my hair."

"Okay. I'll be back with the first aid kit after you get dressed."

I washed my hair and got out of the tub to dry off. Dad had laid out clean clothes for me on the counter. I got dressed and then called my dad.

He grabbed a towel to help me dry my hair before lifting me up onto the vanity so he could apply medicine to my scraped knees and elbows. I hissed out loud. It stung like crazy. I could see how much he loved me by the look in his eyes as he blew on my cuts to try and take some of the pain away.

I felt bad as I watched him. I hadn't lied outright, but I knew that by not telling him what had actually happened, I *had* lied to him.

"Dad…"

"Yeah?" He was still blowing on my scraped up knees.

"Megan and I rode her bike to the beach." There, I said it.

Dad stopped blowing. "Uhh!" He shook his head exasperated. His eyebrow went up. "You did what?"

"Oh no!" I thought to myself but continued to confess.

"W-we crashed when we hit the sand."

"I see." He stood up, towering over me. The look on his face frightened me.

"I-I'm sorry, Dad."

He pointed to the doorway. "Go to your room."

Jumping down, I ran out of the bathroom as fast as I could, fearing the worst. Sitting on the edge of my bed, I waited for him, praying that it wouldn't hurt too badly.

When Dad came into my room, he didn't look mad. He looked disappointed, which is so much worse. I felt awful. I had let him down. "Daddy…"

"Lissy, shh!" He held a finger to his lips to shush me. "You're grounded for the rest of the week: No TV, no computer, no cell phone, unless it's your mother or me. Do you understand?"

"What about Uncle Matt?" The eyebrow went up, and I quickly answered, "Yes, I understand." I was relieved that he had decided to only ground me.

As he turned to leave, he added, "You'll spend the rest of the day in your room, thinking about your actions. I'll call you when dinner's ready."

I just nodded when he looked back to see if I had

heard him. He closed the door as he left my room. "Phew!" I flopped back onto my bed with relief.

The relief was short-lived though. My dad watched my every move the rest of the week. He gave me extra chores each day and never let me out of his sight except to go to the bathroom or to my bedroom.

Finally, Uncle Matt arrived, and Dad let up a little. He even ended my grounding early so I could go to Megan's on Friday. He wanted to talk to Uncle Matt alone. Grown-ups always have ulterior motives. I looked up "ulterior" in the dictionary. It means intentionally (on purpose) kept concealed (hidden).

Megan's Experiment

Megan was in the basement helping Marianna put more liquor behind the bar when I got there. Marianna was complaining in Spanish, and I'm pretty sure she swore. Megan snickered, and Marianna swatted her on the behind.

"Don't you tell Miss Zammy what I say," she warned Megan in her usual broken English.

"That's okay Marianna; I know what that word means." I smiled up at her, and she came after me, arm poised to swat at my behind. I wasn't fast enough, and she connected with a resounding whap. "Ouch!" I grabbed at the seat of my pants and quickly moved out of reach as she swung again for good measure.

"You girls go outside…NOW!"

"What the heck was that all about?" As I rubbed my sore bottom, Megan laughed and shook her head.

"Marianna bought the booze for Mom and Dad's party today. I was helping her carry it in when I dropped a bottle of wine. The bottle practically exploded." Megan snickered again. "She made me put away the booze while she cleaned up the mess." Megan pointed to the wet floor in the kitchen, grabbed a few chocolate chip cookies, and handed one to me as we walked out the door into the garage.

"Let's listen to the radio in my mom's car." Megan had grabbed the keys off the rack by the back door and was sitting in the driver's seat before I could respond. I knew we weren't allowed to mess with Mrs. Jensen's Mercedes, so I refused to touch it, let alone sit in it to listen to the radio. I had gotten into enough hot water already this week.

"Come on, Megan; let's go outside before we get in trouble."

"Chicken?" She dared me with a wicked look on her face.

"Yes, I *am* chicken. I admit it – now come on."

She turned off the car and sneered at me as she put the keys back on the rack. "Catholic girls really *do* start much too late."

"What?"

"It's the lyrics to a Billy Joel song I heard. You've gotta listen to the radio more often Zammy."

"I listen to music."

"You listen to your *dad's* music." Megan ran out of the garage and down the hill to the patio.

"What's wrong with my dad's music?" I asked when I caught up with her.

"Nothing, it's just that there's so much more music out there."

"We listen to other music, too. Just because I don't

listen to the music *you* like…"

"Shh!" Megan started creeping toward the portable bar that had been set up outside on the patio.

"What?"

She shushed me again. The catering crew was there setting up for the Cinco de Mayo party.

"Mom and Dad had to postpone the party until tonight. The caterers couldn't get here until today. My mom was so ticked off."

"Megan! What are you doing?" I was shocked as she started grabbing little bottles of liquor and stuffing them into her pockets.

"We're going to do a little experiment."

"What kind of experiment?" I was getting leery of the way our friendship was progressing lately.

"Don't you want to know what it feels like to be intoxicated?"

"NO!" Why was she so determined to get me to drink with her?

"That's not what you said the other day."

"I said I was curious, but I didn't mean I want to *GET* intoxicated to find out!"

"How are you gonna know if you don't try?" Megan shook her head and ran back up the hill. Reluctantly, I followed.

We raced up to her bedroom, where she hid the bottles in her dollhouse. "My mom and dad would never think to look for these here." She sat back and smiled mischievously.

"Megan, what's going on?" She was scaring me a little. I turned to leave the room to head back home when she grabbed my arm and stopped me. She had an irritated look on her face.

"Hey, you're not thinking about telling your dad, are you?" She squeezed my arm just enough to cause pain and send me a message. I tried to pull away, and she used one of her karate moves to throw me to the floor. Sitting on my stomach, she held my hands above my head and got in my face.

"Promise me you won't tell!" She looked down-right evil. I had never seen her like that before.

"Megan, get off me!" I struggled, but it was no use.

"Promise!" She was nose-to-nose with me.

"You have bad breath!" I started to giggle nervous-ly, and she blew into my face. "Ugh! Get off me!"

"PROMISE ME!" she screamed. She wasn't go-ing to give up.

"ALL RIGHT, I PROMISE! Jeeze! Now get the heck off of me!"

Megan rolled to the right, and we lay side by side on her floor, staring up at the ceiling.

"It's kind of cool…"

"What is?"

"Drinking, Zammy."

"NO!" I cut her off. "End of discussion." I want-ed to leave; the conversation was making me feel uncomfortable.

She turned on her side and stared at me until I couldn't stand it anymore. I finally looked over at her. She was bound and determined to get me to drink with her.

"No! Megan, it's bad enough both my parents

drink. Yours do, too! Why do you want to drink like them? They act silly and do stupid things when they've been drinking. Look what happened to my dad the other night!"

"We won't be driving a car. No one has to know."

"Megan, I cannot – no, I *will not* lie to my dad – my mom either, for that matter! Not ever again!"

"You won't have to. We'll just drink one bottle and see how we feel. You can have the Hypnotiq®. It tastes like fruit punch." Megan got up, took the bottle out, and handed it to me. "It's 34 proof."

"What proof is champagne?" I was thinking about what she'd said the day before.

"Twelve percent."

"You *do* realize it's not normal for a ten-year-old to know this stuff, right?"

"Define *'normal.'*" She took the bottle from me and hid it with the others in her dollhouse. Then, changing the subject, she turned back to me. "Your dad's not angry anymore?"

"I guess not; he let me come over here."

"He didn't spank you?"

"Jeeze, you sound like you wanted him to."

Waving me off with her hand, she ignored my last comment. "Let's see if you can spend the night tonight."

"I don't know, Megan…"

"Oh, come on…"

"Uncle Matt is here, and we might go out for dinner." I was trying to get out of spending the night. I didn't want to drink. Drinking is for adults. Thank God, my cell phone rang, saving me from making a decision.

"Hi, Dad!" It was so good to hear the sound of his voice. "Okay, I'll be right there." I closed my phone, but as I stood up to leave, Megan blocked the doorway.

"Well?"

"Megan, I don't think it's a good idea. I have to go; my dad's waiting for me."

She moved aside, leaving me just enough room to slip by her sideways. "Hey!" she called after me. "We don't have to…you know." She winked at me conspiratorially. "We'll just have pizza and Cokes, okay?"

I thought for a moment. "All right, I'll ask my dad." I hurried down the stairs and ran all the way home. Megan was really starting to freak me out. She was talking about drinking all the time now. I had promised not to tell my dad. What was I going to do? I didn't want to lose my best friend, but she seemed to be going a little too far with this drinking obsession.

Suddenly, Uncle Matt jumped out from behind a tree and lifted me up high in the air. I screamed so loud that he nearly dropped me to cover his ears.

"She's got a good set of lungs, Jaz." That's my dad's nickname. Hey, another acronym, short for 'Joseph Anthony Zamarelli.' Daddy laughed as I ran to him for protection from my uncle.

"Uncle Matt and I are going out tonight. I called Mrs. Jensen to see if you can spend the night. Sound like a plan?"

"You won't be drinking, will you?" Daddy looked sad again, but only for a moment.

"If I do, I'll make sure to get a ride home. Okay, **Warden***?"

"Oh, Daddy!"

He went into the house to get my backpack, and Uncle Matt pulled me into his arms for a hug.

"You didn't even say hello to me when I got here. What's up with that?"

I kissed his cheek and returned the hug before responding. "I was still grounded."

"Yeah, I heard you've turned into a little rebel. How are your knees?"

A prison **warden supervises the operations of a prison.*

"Better. They're scabbed over. Wanna see?"

"Sure." Uncle Matt winked at me and stooped down to get a better look at my battle scars. "Youch! That must have hurt."

"Very much so, sir!"

We were still laughing when Daddy brought my back-pack out and tossed it in the air toward me. Uncle Matt caught it one-handed and held it so I could slip it on.

"See you tomorrow, Monkey!"

"Dad, I'm not a monkey!" I gave him my best stern look, raising my eyebrow like he did when he was angry with me.

"She looks just like you, Jaz."

"Yeah, she does, doesn't she?" Dad patted me on the head like a dog, so I barked at him. I kissed him good-night and walked back to Megan's, wondering what the night would bring and if I still wanted to be friends with her.

Pizza Party

Megan stood in the doorway grinning at me. "You already knew I was spending the night, didn't you?"

Her grin widened as she grabbed my backpack and ran up to her bedroom. I followed, but not too willingly.

"What do I do now, Lord?" I prayed. Daddy says that God always hears us and answers our prayers. *"I hope You're listening."* I thought as I entered Megan's bedroom and closed the door.

"We don't have to drink tonight, Zammy. You just let me know when you're ready, and I'll get the booze. We'll have a regular party."

"How 'bout when we both turn 21?" I looked at the dollhouse, and a cold chill ran up my spine. It was no longer a dollhouse to me; it was evil and haunted. I shivered and looked away. Megan just laughed and turned on the radio. The music was okay, but I really like the music my dad and I listen to better.

Mrs. Jensen called us down to answer the door when the pizza delivery guy got there. We paid him the money she'd left on the table in the foyer. Megan took the tip money and put it in her pocket.

"Megan!" I wondered, *"What's wrong with her?"* I knew about tip money 'cuz I asked my dad one time when he left money on the table at a restaurant and I thought he'd forgotten his change.

The pizza guy was grumbling as he left. Megan giggled as she closed the door and headed to the kitchen. "You take the pizzas up, Zammy. I'm gonna get some glasses for the Coke."

"Megan, you should have given him the tip money."

"I never give them a tip!" She disappeared into the kitchen ending our conversation, so I headed up the stairs.

Mrs. Jensen always ordered a pizza for each of us because Megan didn't like veggies, and I did. "Mmmm…this is so good!" I moaned as we started our feast. Megan handed me a glass of Coke, and I took a long drink from it. "What kind of Coke is this? It tastes funny." I couldn't see the two-liter bottle sitting behind Megan.

"Oh, my mom got that Vitamin Coke for us."

"I thought the Vitamin Coke was diet."

"No, they've started adding vitamins to the regular Coke now. It's new."

I shrugged my shoulders and took another long drink before finishing my first slice of pizza. I reached for another slice as Megan refilled my glass to the top. "Megan, my mom says I'm not supposed to have more than one glass of soda since the other night."

"This is a party; live a little, Kid." She laughed and drank from her own glass. I decided that she was right and took another drink. That's when it hit me. Suddenly, I felt light-headed.

"You okay, Zammy?" Megan asked getting in my face.

"I don't know; I feel dizzy."

She smiled at me knowingly. "Here, drink a little more; it'll make you less dizzy."

The more I drank, the dizzier I got. "Megan! What did you put in the Coke?" I was scared.

"Nothing." She was lying to me.

I grabbed the front of her shirt and pushed her down on the floor. Straddling her, I gave her my nastiest look and asked again, "What's in it?!"

She laughed at me and said, "Vodka – 80 proof."

"How could you do this to me? You're supposed to be my *best* friend!"

"You wanted to know what it feels like to be

intoxicated. Now, you know."

I got off of her, crawled over to the corner of the room, and sat down resting my head on my knees and my hands on my head.

"Hey, don't sweat it, Zam. It only lasts for a few hours."

"I don't like it! I want my daddy!"

"You can't call your dad, Zammy; you made a promise."

"I WANT MY DADDY!" I yelled at the top of my lungs.

Mrs. Jensen came running up the stairs to see what the noise was about. I continued shouting as Mrs. Jensen tried to calm me down. "Megan, what's wrong with her?"

"I don't know, Momma; she just started screaming at me."

Megan began to cry. She was faking it; I could tell.

"I WANT MY DADDY!" I yelled for the ump-teenth time.

"All right, Lissy. Calm down; I'll call him."

Mrs. Jensen took my cell phone and pressed the speed dial for my dad. I could hear her talking to him excitedly. She handed me the phone so I could talk.

"D-D-Daddy…" That was all I could get out. Megan grabbed the phone from me and started running around the room with it. Her mom yelled at her to stop and spun around in a circle trying to catch her.

I started laughing uncontrollably and reached for my glass of Coke before Megan could knock it over. I drank the rest of it and threw the glass against the wall. It made a loud sound as it shattered; glass shards flew everywhere.

Dad had no idea what was going on since Megan had hung up on him and wouldn't answer when he tried to call back. "Something's wrong, Matt. Lissy sounded weird." He called their server over, paid the bill, and they hurried to the car.

"Weird how?" Uncle Matt asked as Dad unlocked the car.

"Weird like she'd had something to drink. She slurred my name. She almost sounded drunk, Matt!" He hastily started the engine, shifted the car into gear, and rushed to the Jensen's house.

Barely able to stand up after finishing my last glass of Coke, I was laughing at Megan. Her mom had finally caught her and was turning her over her knee to spank her. Having never seen someone get spanked, I leaned in close, watching intently. Mrs. Jensen looked over at me angrily. "You're next, Young Lady!"

At that, I turned and ran out of the room, down the stairs, and into the unsuspecting arms of my father who had just arrived.

"HI, DAD!" I yelled before passing out in his arms.

"WHAT IS GOING ON HERE?" My father wanted to know as he lifted my limp body.

"I haven't the foggiest." Megan's dad shrugged his shoulders. He had left the party downstairs to see where his wife had gone.

I came to just in time to see Megan come running down the stairs to hide from her mom behind her dad.

"She's over here, Mrs. Jensen!" I hollered, pointing at Megan.

Daddy lowered me to my feet and looked into my face. "She's stone drunk, for God's sake!"

"What?" Mr. Jensen looked at me, then turned Megan around and looked at her. "So is Megan! EMILY, THESE CHILDREN ARE DRUNK!"

I turned to Uncle Matt, and grinning up at him, I yelled out, "JUST LIKE DADDY!"

"Oh boy!" Uncle Matt shook his head in disbelief as Daddy picked me up again and headed toward the front door.

"We'll talk tomorrow, Sean."

"GOOD-BYE MR. AND MRS. JENSEN!"

"You," Dad looked into my face again, not believing what he was seeing, "keep quiet!"

I started singing one of Dad's songs as he carried me home over his shoulder like a sack of potatoes. Uncle Matt trailed behind a little. He was trying not to grin at me.

Spanked

Daddy was angry - extremely angry! He told Uncle Matt to wait in the living room while he "took care of" me. He wouldn't let me explain what had happened. I didn't know what he had planned until it was too late. He sat on my bed, and before I knew it, he had me over his knee. I cried out after the first whack. Oh, how it hurt! "DADDY, NOOO!" I pleaded with him to stop after he had spanked my bottom the first two times, but he wasn't listening. He spanked me four more times before he laid me on my bed, ordering me not to get up unless I wanted him to give me another spanking.

"I HATE YOU!" I screamed, daring him to come

at me again. He left the room in silence. I was crying so hard I couldn't have gotten up if I had wanted to.

I started to feel dizzy again and called out to Daddy. I needed him. Suddenly, I *had* to get out of bed, even if it meant being punished again. Jumping onto the floor, I ran into him as he opened the door to my room.

"LISSY!" Daddy was furious. Before he could turn me over his knee again, I threw up all over myself *and* all over him!

"I'm sorry, Daddy," I kept repeating, still feeling queasy as he led me to his bathroom and into his walk-in shower. He slid off his shoes before getting in with me, fully clothed. He turned on the water and waited for it to warm up before turning on the showerhead. I clung to him as the water hit me and gasped from the unpleasant shock of it.

Daddy peeled the wet clothes off of my body and wrapped me in one of his huge, warm towels.

Sitting me on his bed, he pointed his finger at me and warned, "Stay put." Then he went back to his bathroom to change into dry clothes.

I was starting to doze off when he came back into the room with dry clothes for me. I just wanted to sleep. This was all a bad dream. Surely it would all be better when I woke up.

Daddy dried me off and helped me into my pajamas.

"Probably vodka, Bro." Uncle Matt was in the hallway gagging as he cleaned up my vomit.

"Yeah, I could smell the alcohol all over me when she puked."

Leaning on Daddy's shoulder, I mumbled another "I'm sorry" before he laid me on my bed and pulled the covers up to my chin.

"I'm disappointed in you, Alicia Marie." He looked really sad. I avoided looking at him because I couldn't stand seeing him so unhappy. I started to cry again and begged him to forgive me. He left the room without saying a word. He didn't even say good-night like he usually did.

"God, are You there? Please answer me! I really messed up this time; I shouldn't have drunk the Coke when it tasted funny. My dad's mad at me. What's Momma gonna say when she finds out? Uncle Matt didn't say anything to me. What am I gonna do? I really need Your help!"

I waited for a reply but heard only the muffled conversation of my dad and uncle as they finished mopping the floor outside my bedroom door. Uncle Matt laughed, and I heard Daddy swear at him. Then they went back downstairs, and I was all alone again.

I got out of bed, but only so I could kneel and pray. Maybe God didn't hear me. I tried again, praying out loud.

"God, please forgive me. Help my daddy to forgive me, too. I love him so much…and…could You make the dizziness go away? I don't want to throw up again; it's so disgusting! Thank You!"

Slipping back into bed, I heard the door to my room open. Uncle Matt crept in and knelt beside my bed.

"Lissy, are you awake?"

"Uh huh," I mumbled.

"I made you a cup of tea. It'll help settle your tummy." He sat me up, and I sipped from the cup as he held it for me. I didn't finish all of the tea, so Uncle Matt left it on my nightstand.

"Thanks, Uncle Matt." He kissed me on the forehead and tucked me back under the blanket.

"Things will look brighter in the morning," he promised as he left my room. "Good night, Sweetheart."

I closed my eyes and whispered another "thank you" to God as I fell into a deep dreamless sleep.

So This Is a Hangover

The next morning, I felt awful. My head was pounding, and my stomach was sore from throwing up so hard the night before. It hurt to open my eyes in the bright sunlight that flooded my room.

"Oh, God!" I groaned as I forced myself to get up and go to the bathroom. My mouth tasted horrible. After brushing my teeth, I managed to walk down-stairs to the kitchen. Uncle Matt was busy making pancakes.

"Well, how's my favorite niece this morning?" He sounded so cheerful – and so LOUD. I held my head and moaned in reply.

"How many pancakes do you want, Sweetheart?"

I shook my head and answered, "None."

The table was cool against my cheek as I leaned over to lay my head down on it. My uncle came over and gave me a big wet, sloppy kiss.

"UNCLE MATT!" I wiped the wetness from my cheek and stood up, slowly. "Where's my dad?"

"He's taking out the trash right now. He'll be back in a few minutes."

"Is he still mad at me?"

"That's between you," Uncle Matt tweaked my nose, "and him." Then he went back to the stove to flip the pancakes before they burned.

I moved to hide behind my uncle when I heard Daddy approach the back door. He didn't come into the kitchen right away, so I went to the door and watched him pull another trash can out to the curb. Turning back to my uncle, I whispered, "My dad spanked me last night."

Uncle Matt knelt down to look me in the eyes and nodded. "I know he did. Do you think you deserved it?" When I looked away, he cupped my chin in his hand, so I had to look at him. "Well?"

Tears filled my eyes as I leaned toward him, put my arms around his neck, and started to sob. I couldn't help it. Daddy came back into the kitchen, but I didn't hear him. Uncle Matt gestured for him to step around the corner, so he could *interrogate** me alone.

Pulling me away so he could look me in the eyes, he asked what had happened the night before and why. I snuffled a little more trying to compose myself while he waited patiently for me to recover.

"I didn't *want* to get intoxicated..."

Interrogate *is to ask someone lots of questions (sometimes trying to get answers or information that the person being questioned considers personal or secret).*

He nodded his head, urging me to continue. I have always been able to talk to Uncle Matt, but this time felt different. I had disgraced myself in front of my father, my uncle, and their friends. Taking a deep breath and letting it out slowly, I began to explain the circumstances that had led up to the previous night's catastrophe.

"Megan and I were talking the day after Daddy got arrested. I told her that I wondered what it would be like to feel intoxicated - you and Daddy do it all the time." Uncle Matt frowned at me when I said that, but he didn't interrupt. "Megan stole some liquor from her mom and dad's bar yesterday and wanted me to try some."

Uncle Matt's expression was suddenly not as friendly as usual. Hurriedly, I explained that I had wanted nothing to do with drinking. "She made me promise not to tell my mom or dad. I was gonna tell *YOU*, but I never got the chance. You and Daddy went out, and I got dumped at the Jensen's house. I really didn't want to spend the night, but I was given no choice."

Tears started to form again, and I wiped them away before they could fall. "Uncle Matt, Megan put vodka in the Coke! I didn't know until it was too late!"

"You couldn't taste the alcohol?"

I could hear the doubt in his voice, but I shook my head. "I've never had vodka. I've never had *any-thing* alcoholic before, so how would I know what it tastes like? I *did* tell Megan the Coke tasted funny, and she said it had vitamins in it like the Diet Coke her mom drinks. I believed her."

Uncle Matt sat me on one of the hard kitchen chairs, and I winced with pain. Apparently, he'd for-gotten about my spanking the night before. I didn't say anything to him and tried to ignore the slight dis-comfort as I sat waiting for him to speak.

"So…Megan spiked your Coke?" Uncle Matt rubbed his chin and looked at me skeptically.

"Spiked? What's that?" I was confused.

"Spiking is when someone puts something in your drink without your knowledge. Did you explain this to your dad?"

The sobbing returned – as usual, no tissues! "No-o-o! He didn't let me tell him anything-g-g!" Uncle Matt took me back into his arms and comforted me as I continued to cry. "I told Daddy I hate him. I don't hate him. I was mad 'cuz it hurt when he spanked me." I started hiccupping. "How am I gonna explain *that* to him?"

Uncle Matt smiled as he wiped the tears from my face and motioned for my dad. "You just did, Sweetie."

Daddy stepped from around the corner, and I ran to him. As he lifted me up, I threw my arms around his neck, laying my head on his shoulder. He rocked me and slowly danced with me around the room. I was his little girl again.

Uncle Matt shut off the stove and winked at Dad as he took a plate of pancakes and headed out to the patio, closing the door behind him so we could have our privacy.

Daddy kept hugging me harder and harder. I gasped when I couldn't stand it any longer, "Daddy, you're squeezing me to death!"

He eased up. "I'm sorry, Lissy; I just love you so much!" He couldn't speak for a moment. "My God, what if you'd passed out at Megan's before her mother had called me? Do you know you can die from drinking too much? Do you?"

I shook my head and rubbed his cheek. It was rough and scratchy against the palm of my hand. "I won't drink ever again, Daddy - not ever! I promise." It was breaking my heart to see him so worried about me. "I'm never going to Megan's again."

"Lissy, I don't want you to give up your friend.

You just have to make the right choices."

"I *did* make the right choice, Dad! I told her no. Megan snuck the booze into my drink – honest!"

Looking into my eyes, he must have decided I was telling the truth. "Booze, huh?"

"Yeah!"

Shaking his head again, and smirking a little, he kissed my cheek. "I believe you, Baby."

Daddy apologized for punishing me without giving me a chance to explain what had happened. I squinted because the pounding in my head was getting worse. Daddy noticed. He gave me some medicine for my headache. After attempting to eat some breakfast, we walked into the living room and began to talk about alcohol and drug addiction.

I asked my dad if he was an alcoholic, but he didn't give me an answer right away. "I don't think I am, Lissy. Daddy doesn't drink all the time. Alcoholics drink every day."

"What about Momma?"

Daddy raised his eyebrow. "What about your momma?"

"I love her, Dad, I do…but…" I stopped afraid to share the truth with him.

"Lissy, what about your momma?" Daddy tried to get me to look at him as he sat down on the couch, holding me at arm's length.

Looking down at my feet, I answered, "She…oh, Daddy, she takes her medicine, and then she drinks a glass or two of wine. I'm afraid she's gonna hurt herself. Sometimes she just sits on the couch zoned-out, and after a while, she goes to sleep." I felt guilty for tattling on Momma. Slowly, I looked up, waiting for him to respond.

Daddy took a deep breath and sighed as he blew it out. He shook his head and looked off to the side. He blinked a few times, but I could see his eyes were starting to get shiny. "I'm sorry, Daddy…" I pulled myself to him and hugged his neck. Daddy wrapped his arms around me and lifted me onto his lap. I didn't have to pull his arms around me for very long before he hugged me tight without my help. "You know, Dad…this is my favorite spot to be in the whole wide world."

Daddy hugged me even tighter. "Yeah?"

"Yeah!" I reached up to stroke his cheek again and he leaned down to rub his other cheek against mine. "Daddy, you need to shave." The sandpapery texture of his face scratched against mine.

"Really?" He rubbed even harder. "Are you sure?" He was teasing me. I giggled out loud.

Then Daddy got quiet. He set me on my feet and looked me in the eyes. "Lissy, I'm going to talk to your momma about mixing alcohol with her medication."

"No, Daddy! She'll get mad at me!" I felt sick again. My distraction hadn't worked.

"Sweetheart, nothing is going to change if I don't say something. I need to make sure you're safe when you go home with your momma. Understand?" I nodded, but couldn't shake off the fear I felt for betraying my mom's secret. I knew she would be angry with me.

"You're not gonna talk to her today, are you?" I didn't want Mom to come and pick me up early from Dad's.

"I'll wait until she comes to pick you up tomorrow. Deal?"

"Deal." I hoped I'd made the right choice in telling him about Momma's problem.

"Dad?" He was wrapped up in his own thoughts and didn't hear me. "Daddy?"

"Yeah, Baby?" He smiled as he came back to reality.

"Megan's parents are alcoholics, aren't they?"

"Yeah, they probably are."

"I don't want to hang out with Megan anymore. What if she spikes my drink again?"

Dad laughed at that but then coughed and took on a serious tone before responding, "I'll speak with her parents. We'll get it straightened out this afternoon. All right?"

"Okay, Dad."

It seemed like everything was going to be okay – at least, that's what I thought at the time.

Making Things Right

After lunch, Daddy and I went to say good-bye to Megan.

"Matt, Lissy and I are going over to the Jensen's house; we'll be back in a few."

Uncle Matt waved to us as we left. He was in the middle of a conversation on his cell phone. Daddy walked with me to Megan's house and spoke with her parents while she and I sat outside on the patio.

The grown-ups weren't talking for very long when an argument began, and my dad called me to leave with him. I heard Mrs. Jensen say, "...lush, just like her father," as I passed her in the living room and went out the front door with my dad.

"What's a lush?" I asked, but Daddy ignored my question. I hadn't had the chance to look up the word in the dictionary yet.

"Daddy?" My dad continued to ignore me; I had to run to keep up with him.

"What's up, Bro?" Uncle Matt wanted to know when we got home. Dad was really upset. He didn't want to talk. I followed him to his office, but he closed the door before I could enter.

"Lissy, what's going on?" Uncle Matt lifted me up.

I stared at the closed door. "Daddy?"

"I think your dad wants some time alone. What happened at the Jensen's?"

"I'm not sure. The grown-ups started yelling at each other, and then Daddy called me to leave with him. Mrs. Jensen called me a lush…just like my father. What's a lush, Uncle Matt?"

"Wow! Sweetie, you and your dad are not lushes.

A lush is someone who drinks all the time. They NEED to drink to feel good. That doesn't sound like your father, does it?"

"No, I guess not. Daddy doesn't drink ALL the time, only sometimes…like when he goes out, or we have company – like you."

"That's right. We'll let him cool off a little. Wanna go swimming with me?"

"YES!"

We changed into our bathing suits, and after we had been swimming for a while, my dad joined us. "BOMBS AWAY!" he shouted as he cannon-bombed us without warning.

Uncle Matt lifted me out of the water and tossed me toward my dad. I landed in front of Daddy and went under. My dad lifted me out of the water and tossed me back to Uncle Matt. Before Uncle Matt could toss me back to my dad, I grabbed him around the neck and held on tight. "I'm not a beach ball!" I yelled.

"Oh, I'm sorry, Lissy. Is that you?" Uncle Matt teased.

We swam until I got hungry and asked my dad to *please* feed me.

"For crying out loud, do you believe this kid, Matt? She wants me to feed her all the time – every day, three times, or more! What's up with that?"

"Daddy, I'm *really* hungry," I joked back. I like it when my dad jokes; he's funny. We ordered pizza, and I asked for water instead of Coke.

"No Coke today, Baby?" Daddy teased. I frowned at him and took a drink of water.

"Ahh, that's high-quality H_2O," I quoted a familiar movie catch phrase. Uncle Matt and Daddy laughed at me, and I forgave my dad for the Coke joke. But I still didn't think it was very funny.

The Nightmare

The next day was Sunday. Daddy and I went to the ten o'clock service at church. Uncle Matt hadn't gone home yet, so he joined us. Afterward, he took Dad and me out to breakfast.

It was nearly one o'clock when we got back to Dad's house, and Dad sent me to pack my bag, so I'd be ready when Momma came to take me back to her house.

"Can I please go over and say good-bye to Megan?" I looked out the front door toward her house.

"*May* I please go over to Megan's?"

"May I please go over to Megan's?" I rolled my eyes, annoyed for being corrected.

Dad frowned at me, but nodded, "I guess so. Don't stay long."

I was out the door within seconds. I wanted to find out what had happened to Megan the night of our "pizza party," since we hadn't had the chance to talk the day before.

Marianna answered the door when I knocked. She let me in and pointed toward Megan's room upstairs before going back to her work. I sprinted up the stairs and knocked on Megan's bedroom door before entering. She was lying on her bed facing the window.

"MEGAN!" I jumped on her bed, but she didn't move. I thought she was asleep – that is, until I reached over and rolled her onto her back. She was staring straight ahead in a weird way. It was pretty scary. I laughed and told her to stop it. She didn't laugh like she usually did when she was messing with me.

Taking a closer look, I realized that something

was wrong. Her lips were a bluish color. Her blue eyes were almost completely black. I shook her several times before calling out to Marianna. When Marianna came into the room, she blessed herself with the sign of the cross and then ordered, "Get the phone! Call 911!"

"Marianna, what's happening?"

I grabbed the phone and dialed the three numbers. When the Operator answered, I handed the phone to Marianna. She was so excited she couldn't speak English and handed the phone back to me. "She doesn't breathe! Tell them!"

As she started to perform CPR on Megan's lifeless body, I got scared and started to cry. The Operator had heard Marianna and told me to calm down. She asked my name, how old I was, and where we were. I struggled to remember Megan's house number; everything was going blank. Looking around the room, I noticed the empty liquor bottles on the floor next to

Megan's dollhouse. There were no bottles left inside it.

Daddy was standing in the front yard talking with Uncle Matt when the ambulance went by. Gasping as it turned into Megan's driveway, they both raced to the Jensen's house.

I was still speaking to the 911 Operator when Daddy rushed into the room with a terrified look on his face. Glancing over at him, I told the Operator, "My daddy's here now. I can hear the ambulance; they're here, too. Yes, ma'am, thank you for your help."

I hung up the phone and tears welled up in my eyes again as I looked over at my best friend. I knew the paramedics would probably not be able to help her. She had felt cold and hard when I touched her. Deep down, I knew she was dead. My best friend was dead at the age of ten from drinking too much alcohol!

Daddy knelt down and held his arms open for me. It felt like I was moving in slow motion as I stepped toward him. He picked me up and held me close. Daddy wanted to take me home, but I had to stay and answer questions for the police. I didn't even notice Uncle Matt standing beside us.

Reporters and photographers were starting to fill the street. I started to shake uncontrollably and someone wrapped a blanket around my shoulders. "She may be in shock; we'll take a look at her." As one of the paramedics checked me out, Daddy stood next to Uncle Matt. He and Uncle Matt had tears in their eyes. I pushed away from the strange woman who tried to flash a bright light into my eyes. I wanted to go home.

"Lissy?" Daddy cupped my chin in his hand and looked at me.

"I'm just c-cold, D-Daddy." I *was* cold and really tired. I didn't know what to think. Emotionally, I *couldn't* feel anything; I didn't *want* to feel anything. I was just numb.

"Okay." Daddy led me downstairs to the living room and held me on his lap. I told the police officers everything that had happened over the past week leading up to the moment I found Megan. They were kind and patient as I tried to answer each of their questions. Finally, the last question was answered, and Daddy stood up with me in his arms to head home.

"I can walk, Daddy," I said flatly. He set me down but kept me close to his body. He and Uncle Matt acted as shields so the photographers couldn't take pictures of me. They kept the reporters from getting in my face, like their bodyguards did when they were on tour.

It took us a long time to get to Dad's house because the reporters wouldn't let us through. They kept crowding in front of us. "Please, let us get by. This

isn't about me. I need to get my daughter home!"
Daddy pleaded. Uncle Matt started pushing them
back so we could get through. He looked angry.

"Matt, Jaz, what happened today?" the reporters
all asked at once, over and over again. Uncle Matt
and Daddy ignored them and kept pushing through
the crowd. I closed my eyes, wishing we were safe at
home. *Why did I have to go to Megan's?* I asked
myself.

Finally, several police officers made the reporters
and paparazzi move back to the street, so we could
walk the rest of the way without being bothered.
Then they stood outside our door until all the strang-
ers went away.

"Is she okay, Jaz?" Uncle Matt asked under his
breath, but I overheard their conversation. Daddy
just shook his head without a reply. "My God, she
just found her best friend dead, Joey! Talk to her!"

"What do I say to my ten-year-old daughter after

witnessing something like that, Matt?!"

"Anything! Joey, she needs to know you're there for her. She needs her dad!"

"I got it!" Daddy snapped. "Look, Katelynn will be here any minute. Maybe it's best if she takes care of this."

"Joey, she needs YOU!"

"I *KNOW* SHE DOES, MATT!" He turned away from Uncle Matt as the doorbell rang. It was my mom. She was there to take me home. Daddy led her aside and explained what had happened at Megan's house.

Realizing that she was there to take me away from my dad, I awoke from my daze and ran to him, locking my arms around his waist. Holding on tight, I cried out, "I don't want to leave, Daddy! Please don't make me leave! I wanna stay here with you... PLEASE!"

"Lissy, it's time to go home with your momma.

She loves you, too."

I shook my head, but Daddy led me outside. Momma picked up my backpack and followed us to her car. As Dad lifted me onto the backseat and buckled my seatbelt, Uncle Matt stood by watching helplessly.

"Katie, call me and let me know how she's doing."

Tears streamed down my face as I reached out to him. "Daddy! I don't want to go…PLEASE!" Dad squeezed my hand before kissing me good-bye and closing the car door.

"Daddy!" I begged, "PLEASE!" I unbuckled my seatbelt and tried to get out of the car. Dad sat me back down on the seat and forced me to stay as he buckled the seatbelt again. I looked up at him pleading with my eyes. I couldn't see through the tears; everything was blurry. "Daddy, please?" I whispered into his ear. "What about Momma's drinking problem?"

Daddy stopped and looked at me. "I'll talk to your mom tomorrow," he promised before he kissed my cheek and backed out of the car.

Uncle Matt leaned in and kissed me. "It'll be okay, Lissy," he assured me.

"No, Uncle Matt, please talk to him! I WANT MY DAD!" Uncle Matt winced as he closed the door and stepped back from the car.

"I love you, Lissy!" With tears in his eyes, Uncle Matt waved good-bye as my mom backed out of the driveway. Daddy looked as miserable as I felt.

Mom stared straight ahead as she drove down the street. She doesn't like confrontations. I was surprised when she asked, "Lissy, what happened?" I ignored her. I didn't want to go over everything that had happened while I was at Daddy's house. I closed my eyes and pretended to go to sleep.

Abandoned

I didn't speak to anyone for the next few days, refusing to answer the phone or come out of my room. Finally, Momma phoned my dad and asked him to please come. Daddy's band postponed several concerts. Uncle Matt was coming, too.

"Lissy?" Daddy spoke softly from the doorway to my bedroom.

"DADDY!" I jumped up from my bed and ran to his outstretched arms. My head hurt from crying. I felt I had lost my best friend *and* my dad when he'd let Momma take me home. I was hungry but had refused to eat anything she prepared for me.

Daddy lifted me up and carried me to the kitchen.

He sat me on the counter while he started putting to-gether a peanut-butter sandwich. Then he took a bite of it. I could tell he was ignoring me on purpose. As he took another bite, he looked down at me. "Oh, did you want some of this?" Winking at me, he cut the sandwich in half, giving me the side with the bites missing.

"Daddy-y-y!"

"What?" He tried to look innocent.

"You bit this."

"I did?" He grinned as he swapped sandwich halves with me, patted me on the head, and then went to the cupboard for glasses. "White or chocolate?"

"Chocolate, please." He knows I love choco-late milk. I bit into my sandwich as he poured our drinks.

"You need to eat from now on, Lissy. Understood?"

I looked away as I took another bite, ignoring him.

He had sent me away when I needed him the most. I was angry.

"Alicia?" He was waiting for me to answer.

"You shouldn't have made me leave. I needed *you*, Dad."

The "sad dad" look reappeared. "Lissy, I thought it was best that you go with your mother and get away from the Jensens after what had happened."

"You didn't call Momma about her drug and alcohol problem," I accused him as I put down my sandwich. I wasn't hungry anymore.

Daddy lifted my sandwich and held it up to my lips. "Take a bite," he ordered with the "strict dad" look on his face. I did as I was told. Handing me my glass, he commanded, "Drink!"

I frowned at him as I chewed the food in my mouth, chewing longer than was necessary. It turned to paste before I swallowed. I took a drink of chocolate milk to wash it down.

Momma came into the kitchen and smiled when she saw that I was eating. She looked worried, but I didn't care. I was mad at her, too. She had refused to take me back to Dad's house, even after I had begged and begged.

She gave my dad a look of thanks. "That's the first thing she's eaten since she came home Sunday afternoon. She wouldn't eat for me." It was Momma's turn to frown.

"Lissy, I don't want you worrying your mother. You need to eat." I couldn't believe it; he was siding with her!

"YOU ABANDONED ME, DADDY!" I didn't mean to scream at him. It just came out that way. All the anger and fear erupted from inside me. "I needed you, and you weren't there for me!"

"Sweetheart!" Daddy picked me up again. I cried as he rocked me from side to side. "I'm sorry, Baby."

"I have nightmares now. I'm afraid to go to sleep."

Daddy looked at Momma. "She never told me about the nightmares." Momma looked hurt.

"You were asleep, Momma. You never wake up after you take your pills and drink alcohol!" I was tired of the secrets in my family.

She looked guilty when Daddy turned to look at her. "Katie, is this true?"

Momma changed the subject, "Joey, maybe she would be better off going back to your place. She wants her father right now."

"Katie, I've got to go back to work. *Is* Lissy safe with you?"

Ignoring his questions again, she responded, "Your daughter needs you right now – to hell with work!"

"Mom swore!" I was shocked.

"Shush!" Dad snapped. He sat me down again and started pacing back and forth. He looked lost and confused. Just then, Uncle Matt walked in and gave me another of his famous wet, sloppy kisses on the cheek. I laughed as I wiped my cheek and slid off the counter to follow him into the living room.

"You know it hurts my feelings when you wipe off my kisses, Little Girl," Uncle Matt pouted as he bent to take me into his arms for a much needed godfatherly hug. "Driving your parents crazy again?" He shook his head in mock disapproval.

"No, they're pretty good at going crazy without my help – thank you very much!"

"Lissy, that's disrespectful!" It was Momma's turn to be shocked. She and Daddy had followed us without my noticing.

I tried to look innocent, but they weren't convinced. "I'm sorry. You weren't supposed to hear that." I pulled myself from Uncle Matt's embrace and turned to hug both of my parents at once. "Group hug!" I squeezed them both tightly.

"Jaz, take as much time off as you need from the tour. Our fans will have to be understanding. Family comes first." He reached over and patted me on the back as I continued to hug my parents.

"Thanks, Uncle Matt."

Ruffling my hair, he turned and went back into the kitchen. I watched him open the refrigerator in search of food. Momma offered to fix him a sandwich, but he refused to let her wait on him. "*I* should be fixing something for *you* to eat." He looked at her with concern. "Your kid's driving you nuts, huh?" Momma just smiled weakly.

I sat down at the table across from Uncle Matt and finished the rest of my sandwich and milk. No one spoke for a while. It was weird. I think they were afraid to talk in front of me.

"Momma…Daddy, would you mind if I go for a walk with Uncle Matt?"

"You may want to get dressed first," Daddy teased

looking me up and down. I did look pretty bad. I cringed as I glanced at my reflection on the shiny refrigerator door.

"Maybe I'll brush my hair, too," I joked back.

Uncle Matt winked at me. "You don't have to get all dolled up for *me,* Sweetie." He can be so goofy sometimes.

"I'll only be a minute." I ran to my room. Momma followed to help get the snarls out of my hair. She wiped my face with a washcloth. I protested as she started to wash my arms also, "Momma, I'm not a baby; I can do that myself."

"Lissy, I just want to help you." She turned away from me quickly. I thought I saw tears forming in her eyes.

"I'm sorry, Mom."

Freshly washed and clothed, I ran and grabbed my uncle's hand, dragging him toward the front door. "Let's go."

I needed to talk to someone. If I tried to talk about Megan, Momma would change the subject – that was, if she wasn't already zoned out on anti-depressants and alcohol. Uncle Matt and I were about a half a block from Momma's house when I looked up at him. He was waiting patiently for me to begin. I could see the concern on his face and felt guilty for all the worry I had caused him and my parents. "Uncle Matt…" I paused not knowing what I wanted to say. I hadn't spoken to anyone other than the police about Megan since the day she had died.

"What's up, Lissy? You know I'm here for you." He nudged my arm as we continued to walk. I *did* know I could trust him. He was like a second father to me. I loved him so much. I could tell him anything and everything.

Turning to face him, I blurted out loudly, "Uncle Matt, it's my fault! I should have told someone about the liquor. If I had, Megan might still be alive!"

He knelt in the middle of the street and held me at arm's length. "Whoa! Lissy, what happened to Megan is *NOT* your fault!" He was serious.

"I should have told…" My lower lip quivered as I tried to hold back the grief I felt. I leaned toward him as the tears overtook me. I wondered, "*What if I had told an adult? Would Megan still be alive? Who knew?*"

He spoke softly into my ear as he held me, "She would have found a way to drink whether you told on her, or not. She was becoming an alcoholic."

I pushed away, looking at him confused. "Kids can't become alcoholics, can they?"

"Unfortunately…yes, they can."

"Uncle Matt, I don't understand. I thought only grown-ups became alcoholics."

"Sweetheart, alcoholism is a form of addiction. It can be passed down from generation to generation. Her parents both drink. No one knew about her drinking, but from the things you've told us, it's obvious she had been drinking for a while and wasn't about to stop. Like I said, even if you had spoken up about her drinking, she would have found a way to continue."

"What's addiction?" I remembered hearing that word during a D.A.R.E meeting at school; I guess I should have paid more attention to what they said about it.

"Addiction is when someone's body relies on a substance, usually alcohol or drugs, for normal functioning. When the substance is removed, it can cause withdrawal." I looked at him confused. He was using a lot of big words. "Withdrawal causes the person to be sick. That's why people with alcoholism get mean or angry. They feel sick if they don't keep drinking."

"Oh!" I finally understood. I nodded my head and we continued down the street. Uncle Matt handed me a tissue. I thanked him. "I asked Momma to let me go to the funeral home for Megan, but she won't let me." I stopped walking and turned to look up at him again. "I'm her best friend. Don't you think I should be allowed to go? I don't know how to convince Momma; she changes the subject every time I bring it up."

"Did your dad say you couldn't go?"

"I didn't ask him yet. Do you think he'll let me?" If anyone could get my mom and dad to agree, it was Uncle Matt.

"Yes, I think he will. He was closer to Megan than your mom was, and he knows how close you and Megan were."

"If they won't go with me, will you take me there?"

"I don't think you have to worry about that, Lissy. Just ask your dad to take you. You know I can't go against their wishes."

I paused to think a moment longer. "Uncle Matt?"

"Yeah?"

"Did my daddy talk to you about Momma's drug and alcohol problem?"

Uncle Matt looked uncomfortable. "Yes, he did."

"Why doesn't he talk to *her* about it?"

"You need to ask your dad that question, Lissy. I can't answer for him." Uncle Matt was shutting down on me. Who was I gonna talk to now?

"Can we go back now?" There was nothing left to discuss.

"Absolutely. Do you feel better?"

"A little bit, thanks." I hugged Uncle Matt again. "You're the best uncle in the whole world." We held hands as we walked back. Daddy was sitting on the front steps waiting for us to return.

"When do *I* get to go for a walk with you?"

"We can go later, after you take me to the funeral home. Okay?"

Dad stood up and raised an eyebrow at Uncle Matt.

"She needs to go, Jaz."

"Katelynn thinks it's best if she doesn't. I don't want to undermine her authority."

"Daddy, I can hear you. Why are you talking in front of me as if I'm not even here? I need to say good-bye to my best friend. Please?"

Daddy frowned but nodded. I could tell he understood. "I'll talk to your mom. You go change into something nicer, a dress maybe."

"I have to wear a dress?"

"Lissy, you should try and dress up a little to show respect."

"A *dress*?"

"Yes, a dress."

"Gosh!" I hated dressing up.

"Watch it, Little Girl!" He gave me his "strict father" look.

"What? I didn't say anything bad." I scooted past him.

"Uh huh," he grumbled aloud, frowning as he nodded his head.

I didn't say anything more. He was going to take me to say good-bye to Megan: Mission accomplished.

Saying Good-Bye

After showering and changing my clothes, Dad drove Mom, Uncle Matt, and me to the funeral home. Mr. Jensen greeted us as we entered. Dad stayed by my side as he and I walked up front. Momma and Uncle Matt stayed behind to speak with the Jensens. Megan lay peacefully in a small white casket with gold trim and angel figurines on the corners.

"She looks just like she's sleeping, Daddy," I whispered.

"Yeah," Daddy whispered back. He held my hand as we stood in front of the coffin.

I started to talk to Megan as if she were still alive,

"I'm sorry I kept my promise to you. I should have told your secret. Maybe you'd be alive right now." Daddy pulled me back from the coffin. I think he was getting nervous at the way I was talking to Megan. I fought to stay. "I'm not done talking to her, Daddy." He stood behind me as I continued, "You better behave when you get to Heaven. God only knows what the angels will do to you." I heard Daddy chuckle, so I turned to frown up at him. "Shh!"

"Sorry, Sweetie," he whispered.

"Dad, can we kneel and pray for her?"

"Okay." He started choking up as we knelt down. I handed him a tissue.

I prayed silently a few minutes before he said it was time to go. I wasn't ready to leave. "I want to stay for the prayer service." They had a wake service for my grandpa when he died. There are prayers, and people get up and share memories.

"Lissy…" Daddy was hesitant.

"Daddy, she was my best friend. I have to stay."

He sighed as he gave in and we took our seats. I sat between Mom and Dad. Uncle Matt sat next to Dad. The pastor from Megan's church talked about life and death, and I zoned out.

Finally, he invited people to come up and share a story about Megan, and I jumped up from my seat. Daddy tried to stop me, but I rushed to the podium and grabbed the microphone unafraid.

"I'm Megan's best friend, Lissy Zamarelli. She's always called me 'Zammy' ever since I can remember." I noticed everyone looking at me but smiled and continued, "Megan and I are…uh…*were* going to be in the sixth grade together next fall. We had the same teacher."

I started to recount the drinking incident, and Daddy came up next to me before I had finished. He apologized to Megan's family, "I'm sorry. She doesn't realize what she's saying. Come on, Lissy;

it's time to go."

"No, Daddy! I'm not done!" I shouted the first thing I could think of into the microphone before he wrenched it from my hand, "SHE WANTED TO BE A STAND UP COMEDIAN!"

I tried to get away from my father. "Why are you doing this?!" I shouted at him.

I kicked him in the shin. He cringed in pain, and I thought he was going to whack my bottom. Instead, he lifted me over his shoulder and carried me out. I started crying and yelled all the louder. "I HATE YOU! I HATE YOU! DON'T TAKE ME AWAY FROM MY FRIEND! MEGAN! I'M SORRY! I'M SORRY!" The other mourners sat in silent shock as we left.

Mom and Dad refused to let me go to the funeral with them the next day. Uncle Matt agreed to babysit me. I ignored him as he tried to cheer me up. When all joking failed, he started tickling me, and I slapped him. I didn't mean to; I just wasn't in the mood to be tickled.

Uncle Matt *did* mean to whack my bottom – twice – before he carried me to my room. I cried as he put me to bed. When Daddy got home from the funeral later that afternoon, he came into my bedroom with Uncle Matt. I thought for sure I was going to get a second spanking from my dad, but I didn't care. I stared out my window as Daddy spoke to me.

"Alicia, you owe your uncle an apology."

"I know." I focused on the squirrel in the tree outside, trying to hide my emotions.

"What do you have to say for yourself?"

"Nothing." I didn't want to talk to any of the adults in my life. I wished they'd leave me alone.

"Alicia Marie…"

Turning toward my dad and my uncle, I felt like exploding. "Daddy I don't know what's wrong with me! I…I…don't know. I'm sorry, Uncle Matt."

My tears returned. "I didn't mean to hit you...I..." Turning back toward the window, I rested my forehead against the cool glass pane and closed my eyes. "Maybe I'm going crazy."

DR. SHAUNA PATRICE, MD

PEDIATRIC/ADOLESCENT PSYCHIATRY SPECIALIST

813

Life without Megan

y freaking out scared my parents so much that they made me go to a counselor. That's what they called her, but the sign on the door read, "Psychiatry Specialist." I *Googled** that when I got home. It's a doctor who treats mental disorders. My parents lied to me.

At first, it felt really weird. I was uncomfortable talking to a stranger. But then I realized Dr. Patrice was okay. She didn't talk down to me like other adults. She asked me to describe how I was feeling. She said

*Google™ *is a registered trademark for the search engine website* www.google.com.

it was okay to be angry, sad, scared, or whatever. She named off lots of feelings. I felt better after talking with her. It was kind of nice having someone to talk to, especially since I was having a hard time trying to talk to my parents. She promised to keep our conversations private, just like Uncle Matt. Going to a psychiatrist wasn't so bad.

We had just come from a session with Dr. Patrice when I asked my dad, "Do I have a mental disorder?" He just hugged me and told me that he loved me, but he didn't answer my question. I thought, *"I wish he'd talk to me!"*

Once I began going to counseling, Mom and Dad started to let me have or do whatever I wanted. I think my parents were afraid I would freak out on them again. They would look at me funny and whisper behind my back when one or the other picked me up. I really wished they would stop doing that and just talk to me!

My dad finally spoke with Momma about the drugs and booze. She stopped drinking when I was home. I don't know if she kept drinking when I was at Dad's, or not. But since there was nothing I could do about it, I pretended I didn't care, so long as she didn't drink when I was with her.

My parents made me go to school again even though there were only a few days left until summer vacation. When I entered the classroom, the kids all turned their eyes away from me. It was like they thought I was carrying a disease or something and would give it to them, and then they would die like Megan.

I overheard some of the girls talking on the playground during recess. They blamed me for Megan's death. I wished I hadn't kept the secret. I wished I'd told someone. I felt so alone.

"Lissy murdered Megan," one of the sixth-graders said to another.

"No, she didn't; she *found* Megan. Megan was already dead."

"Are you sure?"

"The grown-ups think it was suicide."

I should have walked away, but I stayed and listened to them gossip about Megan and me. I got angrier by the minute.

"That's what my parents said. They read it in the newspapers."

"I'm scared to go by her. What if it's catchy?"

"Don't be stupid! You can't catch suicide!"

I had heard enough. I interrupted before they could continue, "Megan didn't commit suicide. You shouldn't talk about people behind their backs because it's rude!" I turned and walked away before any of them could answer.

Mrs. McCurdy asked me to stay after class that day. She wanted to speak with me. We walked down to the teacher's conference room, and I sat across from her and Mrs. Hamood, the School Counselor. I looked up and was surprised when my mom and dad walked in.

"Why didn't you tell me about this?" I asked my parents as I looked from one to the other. They looked at each other and then back at me.

"Sweetie, I told you this morning." Momma started to tear up.

"Oh, I must have forgotten." I tried to make believe I remembered, but I didn't.

I zoned out as usual as they began to discuss my schoolwork, attendance, etc. Boring! When they began to discuss placing me in a special class next fall if my "condition" didn't improve over the summer, I "woke up" and protested defiantly, "No! Mom, Dad, I want to stay with my own class. Please!"

I looked at my dad and realized that I was really seeing him for the first time in weeks – Momma, too. I'd sort of been in a daze for the last month. Momma looked as worn out as Daddy did. They had been working their schedules around mine.

I was sent from the room to wait while the grown-ups discussed my future. I walked down the hallway toward my classroom. The door wasn't locked, so I let myself in and sat down at Megan's desk. It had been left empty since her death the month before.

I don't know how much time went by as I sat there staring blankly. Then I asked out loud, "Hey, God, are You there? You're taking care of Megan, right?"

I looked up when my dad entered the room. He tried to sit facing backwards in the desk in front of me. "That's too small for you, Dad." I looked into his eyes and smirked, and then I let out a long sigh as I turned my attention back to Megan's desk.

Tears filled my eyes as I realized that I would never see my best friend again. "There's no one to call me Zammy anymore; I miss her." A solitary tear rolled down my cheek. Daddy wiped it away and chucked me under the chin. Suddenly, the dam broke loose, and I couldn't hold back the tears any longer. Daddy reached out and pulled me into his arms. I cried so hard my body shook, so Daddy held me tighter.

When my tears finally slowed down, Daddy whispered into my ear, "Let's go home." He paused and then added, "Zammy." I smiled at him.

As we left the classroom, I felt an unexpected release of guilt. All along I had thought it was my fault Megan was dead. I realized that it was not my fault at all. Everyone kept telling me: Grandmama, Uncle Matt, Momma, Daddy, Dr. Patrice – even Dad's girlfriend, Tracey. But it wasn't until this moment that I finally accepted the fact that *Megan* had made the choice to drink – a choice that had ended her life. I felt a sense of peace come over me.

Mom was waiting for us in the parking lot. "Momma, would it be okay if I go home with Daddy?" For some reason, I just felt better when I was with my dad. Mom had started to call me Daddy's Little Girl over the past month. I didn't mind 'cuz it was true.

"If you want to." She smiled and kissed me before I climbed into the backseat of his SUV (another acronym). I put my seatbelt on and waited for Daddy to get into the SUV.

"Don't worry, Katelynn. She'll be fine. I'll make sure she gets to school in the morning."

"I feel like I'm losing her, Joey." Momma looked sad.

"Did you make an appointment to see the therapist?" I overheard him whisper.

"Not yet."

"Do it, Katie, if not for you, for Lissy; she needs *both* of us."

"Okay, I'll call and make an appointment this afternoon."

"Bye, Lissy." Momma blew another kiss and

waved at me before walking over to her car.

"Home, Joseph!" I jokingly ordered as Daddy started the engine. He looked at me in the rearview mirror, and I saw a smile come over his face. I decided it might be a good time to talk to Daddy about some things on my mind.

"Daddy?"

"Yeah, Baby?"

"Can we go to an Alcoholics Anonymous meeting? Dr. Patrice mentioned Alateen for kids at my last appointment. She thought it would really help me. I think I need to go and check it out."

Daddy didn't respond at first; he seemed a million miles away in thought. Then, finally, he nodded. "I'll talk to your mother. Maybe it would be a good idea to go check it out."

Daddy pulled into the driveway and parked the car. I jumped out and opened his door. "What's this, curb service?" he joked and tousled my hair playfully.

"Let's go for a walk." I grabbed his hand and pulled him toward me. Daddy chuckled and allowed me to lead him down the driveway. We walked past a few houses silently before I spoke again. "Dad?"

"Yes, Sweetie?"

"Are you going to see Tracey again?" I looked at him innocently. He turned toward me and shook his head in disbelief.

"You're still worrying about her?"

"Not worried, just curious."

"Curious?"

"Yeah, curious. Are you going to see her, or what?" I wanted to get to the truth.

"That's none of your business, Young Lady." He was grinning and started to laugh.

"It is *SO* my business! Daddy, call her!" I squeezed his hand and yanked his arm.

"Lissy…I don't know." Daddy looked away, then back at me again. I knew he hadn't spoken to Tracey for a few weeks because I had secretly phoned her a few times. She was even easier to talk to than Uncle Matt, although she didn't approve of me phoning without telling my dad.

"Call her, Daddy!" I grabbed his cell phone from his pocket and ran back down the street toward home. Once I found Tracey's number, I pressed the dial key, laughing joyfully when my father caught me around the waist. Lifting me high into the air, he swung me in a circle and then took the phone from my hand as he set me back down on the ground.

"Joey?" I heard Tracey's voice on the phone.

"Talk to her, Daddy," I whispered as I clung to his waist.

He laughed and tried to free himself from my death grip. "Hi, Tracey!"

"Ask her to come and visit," I encouraged him. Daddy shushed me and walked ahead, so he could talk to Tracey privately. I walked a few steps behind my dad waiting for the conversation to end.

Daddy wasn't on the phone very long. He turned back to me, and I raised my eyebrows. He knew what I wanted to know. "Well?" I put my hands on my hips.

"She's – now don't get upset, Lissy." Daddy turned his head away so I couldn't see the expression on his face.

I was starting to get worried. "She's what, Daddy?"

He turned to face me. "She's actually in L.A. and would love to see us," he burst out laughing. I hugged him around the waist again.

"Cool!" I really liked Tracey. She actually seemed interested in whatever I was talking about and didn't interrupt me or try to guess what I was trying to say. Plus, I could tell my dad really liked her. She made him smile; that was the best part! I couldn't wait to see her again. "Oh, Daddy, you should take her out on a romantic dinner date! You should…"

"Whoa, Cupid, slow down! She wants to spend time with *both* of us."

"Both of us? *Really?*"

"I invited her over for the weekend. She'll sleep in the guest room. We'll spend the day with her together. Maybe I'll cook dinner for her. Of course, you'll conveniently disappear into your room because you're so-o-o tired…hmm?"

"Absolutely! Great plan, Dad."

"Lissy…" Dad grabbed my hands in his.

"Yes, Daddy?" I looked up. His eyes were bright and shining as he unexpectedly spun me around and started dancing with me.

"Daddy, people will see." I looked around for paparazzi.

"So what? I don't care. Do you?"

"No, not really." I leaped up into his arms and hugged his neck. Dad carried me into the house.

Glancing back outside, I got a wonderful idea. I took his face into my hands, looked into his eyes, and bounced excitedly begging, "Let's go to the beach and celebrate, Dad!"

"You want to go to the beach *now*?" He set me down just inside the door and stretched his back muscles.

"I want to ride our bikes to the beach."

Daddy shook his head. "Lissy, it's three miles."

"You're not getting too old, are you, Dad?" I teased as I ran from the room.

"You little monkey!" Daddy chased me through the house. I giggled as he scooped me up and started to tickle me. It was good to laugh and be silly again.

At the Beach

After some compromising and a little whining (humiliating, but worth it), Dad agreed to take me to the beach. We changed into our bathing suits; Dad loaded our bikes into the back of his SUV and drove us to the beach. I wanted to show him where Megan and I had crashed into the sand when we had been to the beach on our own.

We pushed our bikes along the boardwalk as I told him about all the things that had gone on the week Megan had died and how I had wanted to confide in him but didn't want to upset him.

Daddy stopped walking and leaned over his bike to take my face in both hands as he spoke, "Lissy, I don't care what's going on in my life. Whether it's going great, or not, I want you to know that you can always, always talk to me. Do you understand?"

I teared up for the umpteenth time since the funeral. "Oh, Daddy! I'm sorry; I was so scared! I wanted to talk to you – I did. But then Megan died, and you and Momma wouldn't talk to me about anything. I thought I was going crazy!" My thoughts tumbled out so rapidly, I was surprised that my dad understood a word I said.

"I'm sorry, Sweetie. Your mom and I were just trying to keep you from hurting any more. We only wanted what was best for you. I guess we were wrong. I'll talk to her."

"No, I want to talk to her myself." I had to work things out with my mom like I had with my dad. I hoped she'd be as agreeable as he was.

"Are you sure?"

"I'm sure. After all, I'm gonna be eleven this fall."

"Wow! My baby girl is growing up." He looked proud.

"Dad, I'm not a baby." I crossed my arms and looked at him sternly.

"You'll always be *MY* baby." He grinned and winked at me.

"I know." I hugged him again. "I love you, Dad."

We decided to park our bikes, so we could walk down to the water's edge. Daddy laid his hand on my shoulder, and I leaned against him as we stepped out onto the sand.

"Dad?"

"Yes?"

"Can I get a motorcycle?"

"What? Where did that random request come from? No, absolutely not!"

"Well, I had to try." I smirked up at him.

Daddy gave me his famous raised eyebrow, and we both laughed out loud.

"Maybe when I'm 16? Sprees® don't cost that much."

"Not even when you turn 18!" Dad was starting to become uptight.

"Daddy!" I nudged him, pretending to be annoyed.

"Come to think of it, never, ever, ever!"

"When I'm 18, I can buy my own." I didn't expect to win the argument, but it was fun trying.

"Lissy…" Dad eyed me strictly.

"Daddy…" I gave him my best "Daddy's Little Girl" look.

We continued to tease each other as we headed toward the water. I kicked off my flip flops, dropped my ratty t-shirt and faded shorts on top of my dad's sandals, and jumped into the waves.

The water was freezing, but it felt nice in the 90-degree heat. Half an hour later, we sat on the sand exhausted and happy. Daddy's cell phone beeped.

"Hold on, Kiddo, gotta get this." He smiled as he checked his messages. "Hmm…Tracey called."

"What did she say?" I wondered, *"Was she canceling on us?"*

"She's coming over tonight." Dad tried to act casual.

"Yay! What time?"

"Let me call her back, Monkey!" Dad laughed at my impatience.

I stood up and hugged my dad around the neck from behind.

"Lissy, I'm trying to use my phone." I had to ease up a little, so he could breathe.

"HI, TRACEY!" I yelled at Dad's cell phone when he started to talk. Daddy laughed and handed the phone to me. He knew I was too excited to stop. "Hi!" I said again, softer.

"Where are you two?" Tracey laughed at my loud hello. She was parked in the driveway at our house.

"I couldn't wait until the weekend to see you and your dad."

"We're at the beach, right down the street."

"Lissy, what are you doing?" Dad looked like he was getting annoyed.

I held up my finger to shush him, and he gave me his "I'm the dad" look.

Ignoring him, I gave Tracey directions. "Dad's car is parked, and our bikes are just down from it… toward the…uh…Ice Cream Shoppe." Tracey repeated my directions back to me. "Yup! Okay, see you soon." I flipped the phone shut.

"Lissy, why did you hang up?" Daddy was *not* pleased with me.

"What? She was at our house. Now she's coming to the beach. We should get our bikes and meet her at the car." I grabbed my clothes and ran toward the boardwalk. Turning to look behind me, I shouted, "COME ON, DADDY!"

He chuckled and shook his head as he used his shirt to brush the sand off of his legs. Dad seemed to move in slow motion as he followed me to the boardwalk. I could barely stand still as I waited for him. I hadn't seen Tracey since the night she went to the movies with us. Talking on the phone just isn't the same as seeing someone in person.

"THERE SHE IS!" I shouted as I noticed Tracey looking toward us. I waved frantically, trying to get her attention.

"Calm down, Lissy." Dad grasped my arm to still me.

Tracey met us as we pushed our bikes up the boardwalk toward her. She and Daddy hugged each other, and then Dad dropped his bike and kissed her. I wondered how they could breathe, they kissed for so long.

"Daddy? Tracey?" I guess they missed each other.

Dad held up his finger for me to wait. When they finally stopped kissing, Tracey came over and hugged me before kissing me on the cheek.

"I'm glad you're not kissing me like you kissed my dad."

"Lissy!" Dad shook his head in embarrassment.

"No, I'll save those kisses for your daddy." Laughing, Tracey turned toward my dad. "You gonna take me for a walk on the beach, Mr. Zamarelli?"

"Absolutely!" Daddy couldn't take his eyes off of her. Tracey had her hair pulled back in a loose ponytail. She was wearing flip flops, cut-off jean shorts, and a teal-colored baby tee that read "Laguna 59" across the front.

We pushed our bikes over to Dad's car and loaded them into the back. Tracey and Daddy held hands as we walked back toward the water.

The sun was very low on the horizon. It was way past dinnertime, and most of the tourists had left, which was great 'cuz I wanted my dad and Tracey to have some time alone. I looked around – no pa-paparazzi in sight. Excellent!

"Stay close, Lissy!" Daddy called back to me as I started walking slower.

"I will." I pretended to collect shells as I watched the two of them walking along the water's edge. It was so romantic. I made sure to leave some distance between us so they could talk. I needed to talk to someone, too: *God.*

I prayed out loud as I followed them down the beach. I kept my voice low enough so that no one could hear me.

"God, I really like Tracey, and I think my dad does, too. Could you maybe help them fall in love? Then my dad will be happy. Please?"

Looking up at the sky, which was turning a beautiful lapis (that was what Tracey called it - her favorite shade of blue), I noticed a shooting star. "Thank you, God!" I smiled and ran to catch up to my father who was looking behind again, motioning for me. He worries too much.

Alateen

We had a great visit with Tracey. It was so nice to laugh and have fun again, to have a girl around that I felt like I could talk to, and to see Daddy so happy. I hadn't seen him smile that much in a long time.

When I told Tracey about Alateen, she offered to go with us. On Tuesday night, we went to the Agape Christian Center. Daddy and Tracey walked me to the room where the kids met. As I entered, I looked at all of the kids standing around talking, and I noticed a table with sodas and cookies on it, lots of chairs, and a podium with a microphone.

Daddy looked even more nervous than I felt.

"It's okay, Dad; I'll be fine." I hugged him and then pulled on his arm until he bent down to my level. "I love you, Daddy," I whispered into his ear. He kissed me and then turned and walked down the hall with Tracey. She joined the Alanon adults as Dad went to his first Alcoholics Anonymous meeting. The judge had ordered Daddy to attend AA meetings and learn about alcohol *abatement** because of his DUI "incident."

In my own group, it was "Open Mic Night." I listened to a few other kids talk about their problems with alcoholic and/or drug-using parents before I got the courage to stand up in front myself. At the leader's prompting, I began, "My name is Alicia Marie; I'm ten years old." I paused, took a deep breath, and continued, "My daddy drinks…"

*Abatement is a disruption in the intensity or amount of something.

Epilogue

It's been almost five months since my dad and I started going to AA and Alateen meetings. My eleventh birthday is in a few weeks, and Thanksgiving and Christmas are coming up, too. I'm proud of my dad. He's been sober ever since the day he got arrested for DUI. He doesn't even drink when he's with Uncle Matt. He has kept his promise to stop smoking, too.

Tracey and Dad are still dating. My father's never been so happy. He spends all of his time off the road with her. Tracey rearranged her book-signing tour to follow MAJIC's tour whenever possible. They're not together every night, but almost. Maybe I'll talk Dad into going to the jewelry store before Christmas. Hmm!

Whenever I need to talk, Dad's there for me – Tracey, too. I talk with Uncle Matt once or twice a week. He forgave me for hitting him that day months ago. I was so relieved to hear him say, "Forgiven and forgotten – just don't ever let it happen again." Then he gave me a real big hug.

I wish Momma would talk to me more. She changes the subject if I talk about something that makes her nervous, which is pretty much everything. Momma doesn't go with us to the AA or Alanon meetings either. She always finds some reason not to go. She still doesn't think she has an addiction problem. But now that I'm going to Alateen, I understand her behaviors a little better. I pray for her every night before I go to bed.

Tracey and Daddy pray with me, too. The Bible states, "For where two or three have gathered together in My name, I am there in their midst" (Matt. 18:20, *New American Standard Version*). Tracey showed me that. She said it means that God is even closer to us when we pray together. Cool, huh?

As extra credit, I wrote a paper titled "Alcohol Abuse by Kids" for my sixth-grade class. My teacher was so impressed with my article that she contacted the local news station. They came to our school and made a big deal about it.

Momma and Daddy came to watch me speak with the reporters. Tracey had to go out of town. Dad promised to get a copy of the interview, so she could watch it with us later. The reporters tried to interview my parents, but they just bragged about how proud they were of me. It felt good hearing them go on and on about me.

Surprisingly, I didn't mind the cameras and reporters like I used to. They were helping me to get out an important message. Maybe together we'd be able to help save a life, and that would definitely be worth the publicity!

Acknowledgements

I offer my deepest thanks to:

...God! Without You, there would be no "Daddy Drinks."

...Mom and Dad for listening to me patiently as I endlessly rambled on about my book.

...Grandma Gates, my godmother, for always believing in me.

...My sister Sandi; my author photo is awesome!

...My sons, Eric and David, and my nephew Matthew for your contributions in creating an amazing book cover.

...My sister Jackie for always being there for moral support and prayer. The illustrations are absolutely outstanding!

…Lori and Jacqui, the two best friends anyone could ever ask for; your support and friendship mean a lot to me. BFF!

…Ron and Diane for being such great friends and neighbors. I appreciate all that you did to help me above and beyond the bonds of friendship.

…Patty, Joanne, Joyce, and Bernie for your moral support and prayers.

…Julie for your suggestions and corrections.

…Deborah, my editor and friend. Thank you for your brilliant suggestions.

…My godchildren: Tammy, Steven, Shauna (I miss you, Sweetie), Alicia, Nicholas, Katelynn, Gabriella, Sean, Emily, and Jacob. I love you all!

In Loving Memory of My Niece & Goddaughter

Shauna Patricia Mikula

August 13, 1985 – August 25, 2005

Daddy's Surprise

The last concert of MAJIC's tour was on my birthday. Momma and Daddy said I could go to the concert since it was on a Saturday night. I was really excited! I hadn't been to one of Daddy's concerts in a long time because I wasn't allowed to stay up late on school nights and most of the concerts were in cities far from home. Tracey was going to be there, too. She and I got to be on stage with the band!

Daddy said he had a surprise for me and Tracey, but he wouldn't tell us what it was. "You'll have to wait until the concert," he teased whenever we asked. I couldn't wait to find out!

I thought Daddy's surprise was a song he wrote

for Tracey. When he asked her to come out on stage, he sang it to her. Tracey begged me to come with her 'cuz she was nervous. I held her hand, and she squeezed so hard I thought my fingers would break. I was a little nervous, too, but it was cool being on stage with the band.

After the song ended, Uncle Matt introduced Tracey and me to the audience, "Ladies and gentlemen, you all know Joey's daughter, Alicia." They cheered, and I waved at them. Uncle Matt continued, "Please also give a huge MAJIC welcome to Joey's new main squeeze, Miss Tracey Helen Gates." Tracey looked extremely uncomfortable as Uncle Matt motioned for her to come farther out onto the stage.

Dad handed his guitar to his technician, then turned and knelt down on one knee in front of Tracey, taking her left hand in his. It was SO romantic! I thought, *"OMG! THIS is the surprise! How could I not see it coming?"*

Tracey's eyes were still shining from Daddy singing to her. She wiped the tears aside and smiled at my dad as he began to speak, "Tracey, I know we've only known each other for a few months…" Daddy started to choke up as he spoke to her. After clearing his throat, he continued, "I can't promise perfection, but I *do* promise to *always* love you and be there for you. I want to spend the rest of my life with you by my side. *Please*, say you'll marry me!"

Tracey gasped as Daddy opened a jewelry box that held the most gorgeous engagement ring. The overhead lights flashed off the solitaire diamond set in a yellow gold band. She let go of my hand and covered her mouth as tears started to stream down her cheeks.

Daddy turned to wink at me and then turned back to speak to Tracey again. "What do you say, Darling?"

Tracey nodded and tried to speak but couldn't get

any sound to come out. Daddy took the ring from the box and slid it onto her finger before rising to tower over us. The audience cheered.

He wiped the tears from Tracey's cheeks and then lifted her chin with his fingers just enough so he could kiss her – right in front of over 50,000 MAJIC fans. The crowd went wild. Tears of joy streamed down my face and blurred my vision.

Uncle Matt hugged Daddy and Tracey. Then he grabbed Tracey's hand and held it up high, so everyone could see her ring. One of the camera-men zoomed in close. We could see the image on the big screens behind the stage. Cheers went up again from the crowd, along with a few "boos" from the broken-hearted female fans.

Uncle Matt held his microphone up so Tracey could address the crowd. Laughing out loud, she pulled my dad and me close before speaking. "I'd apologize for taking him off the market, ladies, but

I'm not sorry; I love him!" She looked into my dad's eyes smiling. "More than life itself!"

The crowd cheered as Daddy kissed her again, and then he and Tracey bent down to kiss me on either cheek. "WOW!" I shouted. "Now, I'll have two moms." I didn't realize the microphone was so close until the crowd shouted again and congratulated *me*!

Tracey reached up to hold my dad's face with both hands. She kissed him once more before teasing, "Go back to work, Jaz!"

Daddy smirked as Tracey and I went to sit back down behind him. He grabbed his guitar and started playing the band's **signature song*** – the last song of the night.

---

*A **signature song** is the one song (or, in some cases, one of a few songs) that a popular and well-established singer or band is most closely identified with, even if the singer or band has had success with a variety of songs.

Tracey hugged me tight and showed me her ring as we sang along with the band. Daddy kept turning to look at us – like he expected Tracey to disappear, or something. As I said before, he worries too much!

- The Beginning -

Sources

Alcohol Abuse

Alcoholics Anonymous

www.alcoholics-anonymous.org

Alcohol Free Children

www.alcoholfreechildren.org

Alanon & Alateen

www.al-anon.alateen.org

Mothers Against Drunk Driving

www.madd.org

Students Against Destructive Decisions

www.sadd.org

(Founded as Students Against Driving Drunk)

AA Regular Meetings

www.aa.org

Drug Abuse

Drug Abuse Resistance Education (D.A.R.E)

www.dare.com

Narcotics Anonymous

www.na.org

Smokers Cessation & Lung Cancer

Quit Smoking

www.understanding-smokingcessation.com

American Lung Association

www.lungusa.org

Stand Up For A Cure*

www.sufac.org

Google**

www.google.com

Wikipedia**

www.en.wikipedia.org

*A non-profit organization dedicated to eradicating lung cancer through strategic partnerships with some of the finest medical institutions in the world.

**Google Search Engine and Wikipedia were used to look up word definitions.